Romara Shaldon
urgent call for hel
had run away with
father had cut Caryl ... sed to
allow her sister to com ... er.

But now he is dead Rom ... ves at Curzon
Street and finds her sister miserably upset and in a
terrible state of fear.

How Romara learns her horrifying secret, how she
is struck by Sir Harvey, and thrown out of the
house, and how one dramatic situation after
another follows this despicable action is told in
the 226th novel by Barbara Cartland.

Also by Barbara Cartland

Books of Love, Life and Health

THE YOUTH SECRET
THE MAGIC OF HONEY
THE MAGIC OF HONEY COOKBOOK
THE FASCINATING FORTIES
MEN ARE WONDERFUL
FOOD FOR LOVE
LOVE, LIFE, AND SEX
RECIPES FOR LOVERS

Historical Biography

THE OUTRAGEOUS QUEEN
THE PRIVATE LIFE OF CHARLES II
THE SCANDALOUS LIFE OF KING CAROL
METTERNICH
DIANE DE POITIERS

Romances

A SWORD TO THE HEART
THE MASK OF LOVE
THE KARMA OF LOVE
THE MAGNIFICENT MARRIAGE
BEWITCHED
THE IMPETUOUS DUCHESS
THE GLITTERING LIGHTS
SHADOW OF SIN
THE TEARS OF LOVE
THE DEVIL IN LOVE
A DREAM FROM THE NIGHT
NEVER LAUGH AT LOVE
THE SECRET OF THE GLEN
THE PROUD PRINCESS
HUNGRY FOR LOVE
THE HEART TRIUMPHANT
THE DISGRACEFUL DUKE
VOTE FOR LOVE
A DUEL WITH DESTINY
PUNISHMENT OF A VIXEN
NO ESCAPE FROM LOVE
THE LOVE PIRATE
A TOUCH OF LOVE
THE SAINT AND THE SINNER
THE PROBLEMS OF LOVE
MAGIC OR MIRAGE?
THE CHIEFTAIN WITHOUT A HEART

Barbara Cartland's Library of Love

THE SHEIK
HIS HOUR
THE KNAVE OF DIAMONDS
A SAFETY MATCH
THE HUNDREDTH CHANCE
THE REASON WHY
THE WAY OF AN EAGLE
THE VICISSITUDES OF EVANGELINE
THE BARS OF IRON
MAN AND MAID
THE SONS OF THE SHEIK
SIX DAYS
RAINBOW IN THE SPRAY
THE GREAT MOMENT
GREATHEART

General

BARBARA CARTLAND'S BOOK OF USELESS INFORMATION

Barbara Cartland

Lord Ravenscar's Revenge

CORGI BOOKS
A DIVISION OF TRANSWORLD PUBLISHERS LTD

LORD RAVENSCAR'S REVENGE
A CORGI BOOK 0 552 10903 7

First publication in Great Britain

PRINTING HISTORY
Corgi edition published 1978

Corgi Books are published by Transworld Publishers Ltd, Century House, 61–63 Uxbridge Road, Ealing, London, W.5.
Made and printed in Great Britain by William Collins Sons & Co Ltd, Glasgow

Author's Note

In January 1793 King George III appointed his son, the Prince of Wales, Colonel Commandant of the Tenth Light Dragoons. Formed in 1715 and previously known as Viscount Colham's Regiment, it could not vie in seniority or martial traditions with the Coldstream Guards, of whom his brother, the Duke of York, was Colonel in Chief. But at least it became the most fashionable Regiment.

George Bryan Brummell, having been given a Coronetcy in 1794, served for two years and was promoted to Captain. In 1794 an Industrial Revolution was taking place and in the North of England idle mechanics were seeking work and, unable to find it, took to rioting.

Troops were used to put down the disturbances, and one evening the Tenth Light Dragoons were warned to be ready to go North on their duties.

The next morning Beau Brummell called on the Prince of Wales.

"I have heard, Your Royal Highness, that we are ordered to Manchester," he said. "You must be aware how disagreeable this would be to *me*."

While the Prince considered the horrors of provincial garrison life, Brummell continued:

"Besides, Sire, *you* would not be there! I am, therefore, with Your Royal Highness's permission, determined to sell out!"

The flattery worked.

"Oh, by all means, Brummell," the Prince replied. "Do as you please, do as you please!"

Chapter One

1807

As the Hackney carriage drew up outside the tall house in Curzon Street, Romara Shaldon saw with relief that there were lights in the windows.

She had been afraid that she would be so late that everyone would have gone to bed and there would be no-one to answer her knock.

The Stage-Coach which had brought her from the country had been delayed by a lot of tiresome incidents, which resulted in its arrival in London several hours overdue.

She had also had difficulty in getting a Hackney carriage at the Two-Necked Swan in Islington.

Those that were still plying for hire were not interested in carrying an unaccompanied woman who was obviously not wealthy and had only a small trunk.

But at last, after what seemed an interminable time, she had reached Curzon Street and found her sister's house.

She had been anxious, in fact deeply perturbed, ever since she had received a letter from Caryl begging her to come to her at once.

It was very unlike Caryl to write in such an hysterical manner, and she thought that even her hand-writing appeared distraught. But the letter explained nothing, merely begging Romara to come to her side, and there was nothing to prevent her from doing so.

Two months ago it would have been a very different story.

Then her father would have forbidden her to listen to anything that Caryl might say, for he had laid it down that her name was not to be mentioned in the house.

It was, in fact, Romara had often thought, her father's authoritative and uncompromising opposition to Caryl's attachment to Sir Harvey Wychbold which had precipitated her into his arms.

There was something fascinating about meeting him clandestinely when she had been forbidden to do so, and although Romara had never liked Sir Harvey she could understand that the sophisticated, much older man-of-the-world would prove irresistible to her sister.

Caryl was lovely, there was no mistaking that, but she knew nothing of life outside the small village in Huntingdonshire where they lived, and had met few men except the son of the local Squire and the friends he brought home with him in the vacations from Oxford.

Romara, although she was only a year older than her sister, had travelled far more.

She had gone on a long visit to Bath with her grandmother when she was taking the waters for her rheumatism, and another year she had stayed with her at Harrogate.

It made her feel in some ways that she was years older and wiser than Caryl, and yet her sister had been brave enough to defy her father's instructions and run away with Sir Harvey Wychbold.

General Sir Alexander Shaldon always treated his daughters as if they were raw recruits under his command.

It never even occurred to him that they might disobey commands he snapped at them, and Romara knew that when Caryl had run away from home, leaving a note behind her to explain what she had done, her father was at first stunned at her audacity.

Then he had said firmly:

"Caryl no longer exists. You will not communicate with her. She will never enter this house again!"

"But . . . Papa . . . whatever she has done, she is still your daughter!" Romara protested.

"I have one daughter and one daughter only," the General retorted, "and that is you."

But now her father was dead, as the result of wounds he had received in the various campaigns in which he had taken part.

So when Caryl's letter came, Romara was thankful that she could answer what she could not help feeling was a cry for help.

"What could have happened?" she asked herself all the time the Stage-Coach was rumbling over the dusty roads.

The horses had moved slowly because as usual the coach was overloaded both with passengers and with baggage.

Caryl would now be married to the man she loved, and after all they had gone through to make this possible it seemed incredible that anything should have gone wrong.

"I am sure I am being needlessly apprehensive," Romara told herself sensibly.

Now as she stepped out of the Hackney carriage she was vividly aware that in a few minutes she would learn the truth and discover how she could help her sister.

The cabman had already climbed down from the box in front of the vehicle to raise the knocker on the front door.

He then returned to collect Romara's trunk.

She thought that his attentions sprang from the fact that he was impressed by the house and that he would expect in consequence a generous tip.

Fortunately, she had enough money to give it to him, and when the door was opened by a liveried man-servant and her trunk was carried in, she thanked the cabman and put the money in his hand.

Then she turned to look at the man-servant to see that he was staring at her with an expression of surprise.

"I am Miss Shaldon."

His expression did not alter and she added:

"This is Sir Harvey Wychbold's house?"

"It is, Miss."

"Then Her Ladyship is expecting me. Will you tell her I have arrived?"

The man looked vaguely towards the stairs as if he was uncertain what to do.

Then at that moment there was a cry and Caryl came running into the Hall.

"Romara! Romara!" she cried. "You have come! Oh, thank God!"

She flung her arms round her sister's neck, holding her tightly in a frantic manner which told Romara that there was something very wrong.

"I am here, dearest," she said quietly. "I am sorry I am late, but the Stage-Coach was as slow as a tortoise."

She tried to speak lightly to relieve the tension, but Caryl, taking her by the hand, was pulling her across the Hall towards an open door.

"You are here and that is all that matters," she said, "and it is better that you have arrived now, as it happens, because Harvey is—out."

It seemed to Romara that her voice trembled on her husband's name. Then they were in a small, well-furnished Sitting-Room and Caryl slammed the door behind them.

"Oh, Romara, you are here! I was so afraid you would not come!"

There were tears in her eyes and her voice seemed to choke on the words.

Romara took off her travelling-cloak, laid it on a chair, and began to undo the ribbons of her bonnet before she asked:

"What has happened? I was sure by your letter that you were upset."

"Upset?" Caryl repeated, and now the tears ran down her cheeks.

Romara put her bonnet and handbag down on top of her cloak and, moving to her sister's side, put her arm round her shoulders.

"What is this all about?" she asked. "I have always thought of you being so happy."

"How—can I be—happy?"

"Shall we sit down and talk about it?" Romara asked quietly. "And if it is possible I would like something to drink. I am not hungry but very thirsty."

"Yes, of course!" Caryl said. "There is champagne here. Would that do?"

"Champagne?" Romara questioned.

Caryl walked to the table in the corner of the room and Romara saw that there was a bottle of champagne resting in an ice-bucket.

There was also a plate of sandwiches, and although she had said she was not hungry, it was in fact a long time since she had eaten anything.

As if Caryl read her thoughts she said:

"The sandwiches are there for—Harvey—but I am sure he would not notice if you had—one or two."

"Not notice?" Romara repeated in a puzzled way. Then she asked:

"Are you saying that Sir Harvey does not know I am arriving to stay with you?"

Caryl handed her a glass of champagne, but as she did so Romara looked sharply at her sister and realised how much she had changed in appearance.

She was still lovely, there was no denying that, but her face was much thinner than when she had left home and there were dark lines under her eyes, which she had never had before.

Holding a sandwich in one hand and a glass of champagne in the other, Romara deliberately walked to the sofa and sat down on it.

"I am rather bewildered, dearest," she said in her soft voice, "so suppose you start at the beginning and tell me exactly why you are unhappy and why you wanted me to come to you."

She took a little sip of the champagne as she spoke, feeling that it would fortify her against what she had to hear.

Very slowly Caryl followed her to the sofa and sat down.

She was wearing an elegant negligé trimmed with frill upon frill of expensive lace, but the light in her eyes, which had given her a sort of radiance, was missing, her mouth drooped at the corners, and there were still tears on her cheeks.

"Tell me what has happened," Romara said coaxingly.

"I—I am going to have a—baby," Caryl answered, "and—and I am not married."

For a moment Romara was paralysed into immobility; then, putting down the glass of champagne on the table beside her, she said:

"D-did I hear you aright, Caryl? You are not... married? But Sir Harvey asked you over and over again to be his wife."

"Yes, I know," Caryl said, "but when we reached London and I belonged to him he kept making excuses, until finally I realised he did not intend to marry me."

"I have never heard of such a thing! How could he behave so despicably?" Romara cried.

"It is not only that," Caryl said in a small, miserable voice. "He is not pleased that I am having a baby and—I think, Romara, that he is growing—tired of me."

Romara put out her arms and drew her sister close to her.

"I cannot believe that is true, dearest," she said. "But he must marry you! Of course he must marry you! I will speak to him."

"He will not listen to you," Caryl said, "and I think he will be very angry that I have asked you to come here. He does not let me meet any of his friends or go anywhere."

"Do you mean to say you just stay here all day by yourself?" Romara enquired.

"It was different when I first ran away with him,"

Caryl replied. "We went to Covent Garden and Sadler's Wells, and we visited Vauxhall Gardens, and it was all very exciting! I loved every—moment of it!"

She gave a heart-rending little sob as she added: "I—loved H-Harvey too."

"I know you did, dearest," Romara said. "That is why I understood, even though Papa was so angry, when you ran away."

Caryl put her hands up to her face.

"Why did I do—anything s-so stupid? Why did I not—l-listen to you and P-Papa?"

Her voice broke on the words and now she was sobbing helplessly against Romara's shoulder.

Romara was trying frantically to think what she should do.

It was too late now, she thought, for regrets. They might have known that, if nothing else, their father was a shrewd judge of character.

He had disliked and despised Sir Harvey Wychbold from the first moment that Caryl had met him at the Meet of the Hounds.

He had been staying in the neighbourhood and had insisted on his host introducing him to Caryl, and from that moment he had pursued her indefatigably.

He had sent her notes and flowers and had called daily, until the General had turned him out of the house. Then he had inveigled Caryl into meeting him in secret.

Romara could understand how fascinating it had been to a girl who had never received such fulsome compliments to be made love to by a man who was extremely experienced in the art of seduction.

But it still astounded her that Sir Harvey, who was a gentleman by birth, should have gone back on his promise to marry Caryl and reduced her to this state.

As her father was dead, it was now her duty to try to rouse Sir Harvey to a sense of his responsibilities, but nevertheless her heart sank at the thought.

"Stop crying, dearest," she said to Caryl, "and tell me when Sir Harvey is likely to return."

"I—I have—n-no idea," Caryl answered. "S-sometimes he stays out until d-dawn—and I think he is with—a woman who—attracts him m-more than I d-do."

Her words brought on another tempest of tears, and Romara could do nothing but hold her closer and wish as she had never wished before that her father were alive.

"I did not know—what to do," Caryl said when she could speak coherently, "except to ask you to help me. Perhaps I should have—c-come home—but I have no—money."

"No money!" Romara exclaimed.

"Harvey never gives me any to spend, and I am not allowed to go shopping without him."

Romara thought that her sister was certainly being kept a prisoner. At the same time, she was obviously surrounded by luxury.

If she went home it would be very difficult to explain her circumstances to the village and the neighbourhood—that she was to have a baby and was not married.

Something of her father in Romara made her swear to herself that she would compel Sir Harvey to fulfil his obligations, but she had no idea how it would be possible.

She wondered wildly if they had any relations to whom Caryl could turn for help.

Their grandmother was dead and the General had in fact been an only child, while their mother's relatives all lived in Northumberland.

"How long is it before your baby is due?" Romara asked.

"I—I think in about—two months," Caryl answered.

Romara looked surprised.

"It does not show very much," Caryl said, "and Harvey bought me special gowns to disguise my figure."

That was the reason, Romara thought, that she had not noticed the moment she arrived that Caryl had changed. The negligé was full and floated round her.

Now as she looked at her sister more closely she knew that to an experienced or curious eye it was quite obvious that she was not the slim, graceful girl she had been when she had left home.

"I have been worrying about the—baby," Caryl said almost in a whisper. "Harvey has not let me buy any—clothes for it, not even a shawl. I keep wondering whether, since he dislikes the idea, he will let me have it here in this house."

"Where else does he expect you to have it?" Romara enquired.

"I do—not know. H-he does not—like babies."

She was crying again and Romara thought helplessly that the tangle in which her sister was involved seemed to be getting worse every moment.

"Stop crying, Caryl dear," she pleaded.

"I l-loved Harvey—and now that he does not—love me any more, I—do not know—what to do."

It would be difficult for anyone to love such a monster, Romara thought privately, but she was wise enough not to express her thoughts out loud.

Instead, she took her handkerchief and wiped Caryl's cheeks, then made her sip a little champagne.

"I hate champagne!" Caryl said petulantly. "When I first came away with Harvey I drank a lot of it because he wanted me to, but now it makes me feel sick!"

"Then shall I ring for some coffee for you?" Romara asked. "Or perhaps some warm milk? You know we always had to drink that as children when we were upset."

"No! No!" Caryl cried quickly. "The servants will think it strange. I do not want them to know about my condition."

"But surely they must guess?" Romara questioned.

"Only my lady's-maid knows, and she is a kind woman and I think loyal to me," Caryl answered.

Romara thought that if she knew anything about servants, her lady's-maid would not have kept secret such a momentous event.

But she saw that Caryl was frightened of everything and everybody and she knew that this was not the moment to try to make her resolute.

The whole trouble had always been, Romara thought, that Caryl was easily led and appeared to have little will of her own.

It was certainly not her sister who had made the decision to run away, but she would not have had the strength to resist the blandishments by which Sir Harvey would have persuaded her into doing exactly what he wished.

'What shall I do? What can I do about it?' Romara was asking herself silently.

She had not met Sir Harvey many times because after the General had forbidden him into the house Caryl had gone alone to their secret rendezvous.

She remembered him as good-looking in a rather florid way, very elaborately dressed, and having a bold look in his eyes which always made her feel embarrassed.

Her father had not volunteered much information as to why he disliked Sir Harvey enough to forbid him to court his younger daughter.

But when the General had read the letter that Caryl left behind, he had said in a tone of utter contempt:

"That libertine! That lecher!"

Then he had thrown down the letter and made his declaration that Caryl was no longer his daughter.

He must have known something against Sir Harvey to make him take such an attitude, and Romara could only think now how right he had been.

Because Caryl seemed almost exhausted by her tears, Romara took the initiative by rising to her feet.

"It is getting very late, dearest," she said, "and as you have no idea what time Sir Harvey will be returning, I suggest we go to bed and break the news of my arrival to him in the morning."

"I warn you, Romara—he will be—angry. He will be very—angry!"

"I am not afraid," Romara said firmly, although it was not quite the truth.

She put out her hand to Caryl and as she did so there was the sound of voices in the Hall and Caryl gave a little cry of sheer fear.

"It is—Harvey!" she whispered almost beneath her breath. "H-he has—returned!"

"Well, that makes it easier," Romara said quietly. "I can see him now and tell him why I have come."

At the same time, she felt a little tremor within herself not exactly of fear but of unease about the interview, which she knew was going to be difficult and unpleasant.

The door to the Sitting-Room was flung open and Sir Harvey stood there resplendent in evening-dress, his face very red above a high cravat, an unmistakable expression of anger in his eyes.

He stood for a moment in a theatrical attitude, staring at the two women standing side by side.

Caryl gave a little cry that was childish. Then she said in a quivering voice:

"Y-you are—b-back—H-Harvey!"

"That is obvious!" he snapped.

Then with his eyes on Romara he asked:

"What the devil are you doing here?"

"I have come to see my sister," Romara answered quietly, "which is hardly surprising . . . in the circumstances."

"What circumstances?" Sir Harvey questioned.

He spoke the last word in a manner which made Romara think he had been drinking.

He was not drunk, but undoubtedly the wine had inflamed not only his face but the rising anger that she sensed he was feeling.

He walked towards them both, then when he reached them he addressed Caryl.

"If I have told you once I have told you a dozen times," he said, "that you are not to speak to anyone without my permission, and certainly not to tell them of the disgusting state you are in."

"Oh—Harvey—it is not—m-my fault."

"Then whose fault is it?" he asked. "Will you learn to keep your mouth shut, you snivelling little fool?"

As he spoke he raised his hand and slapped Caryl across the face so hard that she fell onto the sofa from which she had just risen.

"How dare you!" Romara cried. "How dare you strike my sister!"

She diverted Sir Harvey's attention from Caryl to herself.

"I shall do as I like," he retorted. "And who is going to stop me?"

"I am!" Romara declared. "And I intend to make you marry Caryl as you promised to do."

"And how are you going to do that?" Sir Harvey enquired menacingly.

"Unless you marry her, I will see that your behaviour is known to your friends and to everyone of consequence in London. If necessary, I will petition the Queen herself on Caryl's behalf."

Romara spoke fiercely but distinctly, her eyes blazing with anger, her face very pale, but she held herself proudly and her voice seemed to ring out like a clarion call.

"And you think, you little vixen, that you can interfere in my life?" Sir Harvey shouted. "If you say one word against me in public I will kill you for it—make no mistake—I will kill you!"

As he spoke he clenched his fist, drew his arm back, and punched Romara straight in the face.

She staggered and fell to her knees, while Caryl screamed and screamed again.

As if the sound of it made Sir Harvey lose all control, he pulled Romara up from the floor, punched her again, and then, dragging her by the arm, pulled her across the room.

As he reached the door he saw her bonnet, cloak, and handbag on the chair and picked them up with his free hand.

Then he went on towards the front door, with

Romara, dazed and half-blind, stumbling over her feet.

There was a footman in attendance, who looked at his Master in horror.

"Open that door, Thomas!" Sir Harvey shouted, and the man hurried to obey.

The door was opened and he flung Romara through it with all his strength. She fell on the steps, rolled down the last one, and lay still on the pavement.

Sir Harvey flung her things after her, with the handbag hitting her on the head. Then he surveyed her from the open doorway with satisfaction.

"That'll teach you a lesson you'll not forget in a hurry!" he shouted.

He slammed the door and the footman locked and barred it.

* * *

Romara must have been unconscious for some minutes when down the steps of the house next door to Sir Harvey's a number of smartly dressed gentlemen descended rather carefully, two of them obviously unsteady on their feet.

"Where'll we start to look?" one of them asked.

"Where do you sugges'?" another replied.

It was obvious that both of them were having some difficulty in speaking distinctly.

"We have to shurry," a third said. "It'll shpoil all the fun if Trent changes his min'."

"He shwore what he swould do," someone answered, "an' Trent ish a man of his word! I tell you—Trent ish a man of his word!"

"Well, come on then. What are we waiting for?"

The speaker braced himself to start walking down Curzon Street, then saw Romara lying on the pavement in front of him.

"What have we here?" he asked.

"It looksh like a woman," a friend said blithely.

"Of course it'sh a woman, you fool! But why'sh she lying here?"

"P'raps she's tipshy," one of the other men suggested.

"Looks as though she's been in a fight," someone said. "Her face is bleeding."

The first gentleman peered a little closer.

"She looks a fright!" he said.

Then he gave an exclamation.

"My God! Thish's jus' what we're looking for!"

"What—her?"

"Take a look at her. Did you ever see anyshing sho—ugly?"

A kind of whoop went up from the other gentlemen crowding round.

"Uglies' woman in London, he said, and that'sh what we have found!"

"Then we will shtake her back. Pick her up."

It was with some difficulty that the gentlemen carried Romara, since they were hardly able to carry themselves. But they managed to lift her off the pavement.

One eye was open and she appeared to have regained consciousness by the time they had carried her up the steps of the house they had just left and into the marble Hall.

"Ish Trent swhere we left him?" someone asked.

"I 'spect he is. Le'sh find out."

With their arms round Romara, her feet dragging on the carpet, they got her down a wide corridor which led to the Dining-Room.

Seated at the far end of the table, his head resting on one hand, the other holding a glass of brandy, was a young man.

Beside him, replenishing his glass from a decanter every time it emptied, was a rather foolish-looking gentleman who was extremely "foxed."

He had difficulty in perceiving that his friends, who had left the table only a few minutes ago, had returned.

"What—have you—got—there?" he enquired.

"The woman we swere looking for," one of the gentlemen supporting Romara answered. "We hadn't to go far, sfortunately, as God or perhaps those angels you're always blabbering about, Joshua, had put her down on the door-shtep!"

"Angels? What—angels?" Joshua questioned vaguely.

"Oh, sober him up, someone!" commanded the gentleman with his arm round Romara.

"If you ask me, he's too bottled to 'member the Shervice," someone said.

"I can take any Shervice," Joshua replied in affronted tones. "Any Shervice you like. I'm a Parshon! Who shays I'm not a Parshon?"

"All right, ol' boy, we know you're a Parson," the first gentleman replied. "It'sh the Weddin'-Service we want. Can you 'member the words?"

"O' courshe I can—remember the—words! Who shays I—can't?"

"No-one! No-one!" everybody said hastily. "Come on, then. Tell Trent his bride's here."

At the sound of his name the man sitting at the end of the table raised his head.

"What's happening? What are you all talking about?" he demanded.

He spoke in a clearer and less inebriated tone than any of the others.

"We've found what you wanted, Trent. Ugliest woman in London! Are you going t' marry her, as you said you shwould? Or are you going back on your word?"

"Trent's a man o' his shword," someone piped up. "That'sh wha' I say—and I'll shay it again—Trent's a man of his word!"

"Of course I meant what I said," Trent replied. "I intend to show that damned woman I am not to be played with, and I'll be married before she is! That is what I said, and that is what I will do!"

"Then you can be smarried now. We've your bride with ush. Look at her, Trent. You couldn't find an uglier woman anywhere!"

"The uglier the better!" Trent replied, and his voice was deep with anger.

"Come on, Joshua," cried someone. "You'll have to shtand up. We'll give you a chair to suppor' you."

"As the gentleman spoke he turned one of the high-back chairs round and two other men propped Joshua against it.

"Do you wan' a Prayer-Book?" one of them asked.

'I know the—wordshs!" Joshua said with drunken dignity.

"What's th' bride'sh name?"

There was a moment's consternation. Then the last man to enter the room was seen to be carrying Romara's cloak, bonnet, and handbag, which he had picked up from the pavement.

Someone opened the handbag and spilled out what it contained on the table.

There were three gold sovereigns, some small change, a handkerchief, a key, and a letter.

A gentleman took up the letter and peered at it with bleary eyes.

"Swhat's it—say?" he asked.

"It's—addressed to—Miss Romara Shaldon!" he answered with difficulty.

"Then that's her name!" his friend cried. "Stands to reason she swouldn't be carrying round a letter to shanyone elshe!"

"Romara—never heard the name—before."

"That doeshn't matter! Joshua—are you listening? Joshua—the bride's name is Romara."

"Ro-mar-a," Joshua repeated slowly.

"Leave him alone—he'll be all right," someone else said. "Make Trent shtand beside the bride."

With some difficulty they got them together.

One of Romara's eyes was closed where Sir Harvey had hit her. The other seemed to be staring fixedly ahead at nothing.

Blood was running from her nose down to her chin and there was a huge gash on one side of her mouth, which was also bleeding.

Sir Harvey's signet-ring had cut her cheek the second time he had hit her and there was an open wound.

Her hair had come unpinned and was falling down her neck.

She looked grotesque, and yet it seemed from

the expressions of those looking at her that she was exactly what they wanted.

Slowly and surprisingly accurately, considering the state he was in, Joshua began the Marriage-Service....

* * *

Lord Ravenscar stirred and groaned.

His Valet, who was tidying the bed-room, came to his side.

"Is there anything I can get you, M'Lord?"

"Yes, you fool! Coffee, and an ice-pack for my head."

"It's here, M'Lord."

The Valet turned to the wash-hand-stand and came back with an ice-pack, which he laid gently on his Master's forehead.

Then he poured out a large cup of black coffee from the silver coffee-pot which stood on a side-table by the bed.

"Shall I lift your head, M'Lord?" he asked.

Lord Ravenscar groaned again and said:

"I will manage."

He sat up, aware that his head hurt him intolerably as he did so, but conscious that even for the few seconds the ice-pack had been on his head it had helped.

He drank the coffee off at one gulp and lay down again, adjusting the ice-pack.

After a moment he said:

"I have a feeling, Hignet, that I was a trifle 'botski' last night."

"Not a trifle, M'Lord. I've never known you so 'dipped'!"

"Must have been the brandy," Lord Ravenscar said reflectively. "It was good brandy—excellent brandy—but I had too much of it!"

"Too much indeed, M'Lord," Hignet agreed.

Lord Ravenscar was silent and Hignet busied himself with arranging his Master's clothes on a chair and setting beside them a pair of Hessian boots.

These were polished in a manner which the Valet was aware was the envy of every other Beau in the whole of St. James's.

In fact, quite a number of his Master's friends had tried to bribe him into disclosing the secret of the special polish that he had invented, but Hignet was loyal and he was also extremely proud of the Nobleman he served.

"Hignet!"

It was Lord Ravenscar's voice, coming from the bed.

The Valet came to his side.

"Yes, M'Lord?"

"I have a feeling that something happened last night."

"It did, M'Lord."

"What was it?"

"Your Lordship has no idea?"

"If I had, I should not ask you."

"No, M'Lord."

There was silence. Then Lord Ravenscar said:

"I am waiting to hear the worst."

"You were—married, M'Lord!"

For a moment Lord Ravenscar did not move a muscle, then he said quietly:

"That is what I—suspected had occurred."

Now it was all coming back to him, that moment when Atalie had been waiting for him in a Salon of her father"s house in Berkeley Square.

He had received her note early in the morning and had waited with the utmost impatience until five o'clock in the afternoon, when she had asked him to call on her.

He could remember how eagerly he had hurried up the stairs to the Salon on the first floor and found that she was alone, looking lovelier, he thought, than he had ever seen her.

Atalie Bray had taken by storm London and the hearts of the gentlemen who prided themselves on their discriminating taste.

Her beauty was sensational even by the standard of beautiful women set by the Duchess of Devonshire, Lady Jersey, and the Countess of Bessborough.

She managed to make them look like overblown roses beside a white orchid so exquisite, so unusual, that even those like Lord Ravenscar, who had grown blasé and cynical, were swept off their feet.

In fact, Lord Ravenscar had fallen in love for what he believed to be the first and only time in his life.

At least, although he had had numerous love-affairs, as was not surprising with his looks and wealth, he had never asked anyone to marry him and he had been quite sure that Atalie would appreciate the compliment he paid her.

She had in fact made it very plain that she reciprocated his affection.

At the same time, she asked him to wait a short while so that they would get to know each other a little better.

Infatuated and bemused by her beauty, he was prepared to agree to anything she wanted so long as she eventually became his wife.

It was not surprising that he did not for a moment suspect that she might not be as enraptured at the thought of bearing his name as he was of possessing her.

Atalie Bray, although she was amazingly beautiful, had little else to recommend her.

Her father was not aristocratic in any sense of the word, although he was a gentleman of good breeding.

It was entirely due to her looks that Atalie was acclaimed by the *Beau Monde* and was accepted into the exclusive set that surrounded the Prince of Wales at Carlton House.

He was aware that as Lord Ravenscar's wife every door in the Social World would be open to her for the rest of her life, and her position in the land would be the envy of every other marriageable young woman and certainly their ambitious mothers.

Confident that he had obtained his heart's desire, and having not a single doubt that his happiness was assured for all time, Lord Ravenscar had thought when Atalie sent for him that she intended to tell him that she was prepared for their engagement to be announced to their friends and published in *The Gazette*.

She turned her face towards him as he walked across the Salon.

Lord Ravenscar was possessed by the desire to kiss her until she was breathless and pour out once again the passionate plea that they should be married as soon as possible.

How could he wait for her? How could he possess himself in patience until this lovely creature was his completely?

But even as he reached her side and put out his arms Atalie help up one of her slim graceful hands to stop him.

"Wait, Trent," she said. "I have something to tell you."

"It is not important," Lord Ravenscar replied. "Let me kiss you first and we can talk afterwards."

"No," she answered. "There is something you have to hear."

He was not interested, but to please her Lord Ravenscar waited, with a smile on his lips, his dark eyes devouring her loveliness, thinking that no-one could look more exquisite or more unusual.

He had already planned in his mind the jewellery he would give her once she was his wife.

Diamonds that would sparkle like her eyes, pearls to flatter the translucence of her skin, rubies to express the fire that burnt within him every time he touched her.

Lastly, emeralds, because they held a mystery which seemed to echo the mystery in her eyes.

"Tell me! Tell me quickly!" he said at length as Atalie did not speak.

"I am afraid you will be somewhat upset, Trent," she said coolly, "but last night I accepted Hugo Chester!"

He knew the Marquis of Chester—a pleasant but rather stupid young man who had only recently become a member of White's Club.

"I mean that I am to marry him," Atalie said.

Lord Ravenscar stared at her in stupefied bewilderment, thinking that something must be wrong with his hearing.

It was impossible, completely impossible, that Atalie, his Atalie, should have said such a thing.

As if she had some sympathy for what he was feeling, she said a little more gently:

"I am sorry, Trent. I am fond of you, and I think we should have dealt well together, but Hugo will eventually be a Duke and I do so want to be a Duchess."

For a moment it crossed Lord Ravenscar's mind that it would be easy, very easy, to kill her, but without saying a word he turned and walked slowly down the stairs up which he had just run so eagerly.

Taking his hat and stick from a servant, he went out into Berkeley Square and walked.

He had no idea now where he had gone.

He only remembered that eventually he found his way home to discover he had forgotten that he had invited several of his friends to dinner.

They were waiting for him and they stared in astonishment when he came into the room unchanged and with a look on his face which made their protestations and questions die on their lips.

It was then, Lord Ravenscar thought now, that he had begun to drink.

As he did so he listened to the commiserations of his friends and was aware of an anger within himself which had been increasing since the moment he had thought he might kill Atalie.

The Ravenscars were noted for their quick tempers and he had often thought that the Christian name his father has chosen for him, which meant "Swift," was indicative of his rather dry humour.

"Swift by name, and swift by nature, that's you, Master Trent," his Nurse had said over and over again when he got into one of his tantrums.

But if they were swift to come they were usually swift to go, though now, Lord Ravenscar thought bitterly, his anger of last night had lasted long enough for him to make a fool of himself.

He could recall drinking and drinking all through dinner and being unable to eat any of the dishes his Chef had prepared.

Then someone—he thought perhaps it was Anthony Garson—had asked him what he was going to do.

"I have thought what I am going to do," he had replied slowly in a voice which vibrated with anger.

"What is that?" a number of his guests asked.

"I am going to show Atalie Bray that she is not the only person who can get married," he answered.

"What do you mean by that?" Anthony enquired.

Lord Ravenscar remembered choosing his words with extreme care.

"I shall get married before she does," he replied, "and before her engagement is even announced!"

"Do you mean so that everyone will think you have jilted her?" his friend Anthony asked with surprising clarity of mind, considering the circumstances.

"Exactly!" Lord Ravenscar said. "And I shall marry deliberately, and I swear it, the ugliest woman I can find."

At this there was a shout which echoed round the Dining-Room.

Lord Ravenscar raised his glass.

"To my wife!" he said. "The ugliest woman in London, whom I preferred to the most beautiful!"

His mind might be hazy with drink, but he thought with satisfaction that his revenge would be the delight of the cartoonists and the gossip-writers, who were only too pleased to be scurrilous about anybody of the *Ton.*

The gossip would hurt Atalie as she had hurt him, which was what he intended.

It was Viscount Garson who had been only too ready to translate his words into action.

"You are right, Trent," he agreed. "That is exactly what you must do. Show Atalie what happens when she jilts a man like you for a mere title."

He looked at the flushed faces round the dining-table and added:

"What are we waiting for? Let ush go and find

the ugliest woman in London so that Trent can marry her here and now before anyone learns of Atalie's engagement to Cheshter."

"Of course!" several of the gentlemen had cried.

"As Joshua is here, he can marry them."

The Viscount pointed as he spoke towards the Honourable Joshua Meeding, who was one of Lord Ravenscar's most devoted admirers.

He was always to be found at every social function when he was not at White's Club, but he had in fact been ordained as a Parson.

The youngest son of Lord Meed, he had gone into the Church because that was the family tradition, his eldest brother being in the Army and his second in the Navy.

But Lord Meed had unexpectedly come into a great fortune, and, there being no need therefore for any of his sons to earn their living, Joshua was a Parson without a Parish and a "Gentleman-About-Town."

It was unfortunate, Lord Ravenscar thought now, that Joshua had been dining with him that evening of all nights.

If he had not been there it would have given him time to sober up and decide that even revenging himself on Atalie was not worth the sacrifice of his freedom.

He was still angry with her, still humiliated by the fact that she had turned him down after promising to be his wife, but as always when his temper abated the fury went out of him.

Now he felt only a bitterness which he knew would make him more cynical about women than he was already.

How could he have imagined for one moment that Atalie, with all her beauty, was any different from all the other creatures which he had found after a time were either bores or liars?

Invariably their lack of brains was not compensated by their more obvious physical charms.

'I have made a damned fool of myself,' Lord Ravenscar thought, and aloud he said:

"Hignet!"

"Yes, M'Lord?"

"Where is the lady I married last night?"

"Mrs. Fellows is looking after her, M'Lord. The lady must have had some sort of accident."

There was a note in Hignet's voice which told Lord Ravenscar, who knew him so well, that he had more to say.

"What was the accident, Hignet?" His Lordship enquired.

The Valet hesitated for a moment, then he said:

"It's only what I've ascertained, M'Lord, when I happened to be speaking to Mr. Feltham, who's Butler to Sir Harvey Wychbold, next door."

"And what had Feltham to do with the accident?"

"Not Mr. Feltham, M'Lord—Sir Harvey!"

Lord Ravenscar waited.

He knew that Hignet was an incorrigible gossip and it was only a question of time before the information he was longing to impart would burst from him.

"Mr. Feltham said, M'Lord, that the young lady who's now here in this house arrived late last night at Sir Harvey's residence. . . ."

"You're not telling me, Hignet, that I have married one of Wychbold's cast-offs?"

There was a note in Lord Ravenscar's voice which made his Valet say quickly:

"No, no, M'Lord! She had nothing personally to do with Sir Harvey, having only just arrived, so to speak. But it seems he took some exception to her."

"What do you mean by that?" Lord Ravenscar enquired.

"Sir Harvey punched her in the face, M'Lord, and threw her down the front steps. That would account for the fact that Mrs. Fellows tells me the lady's still unconscious!"

"Unconscious?" Lord Ravenscar repeated. "You tell me that Wychbold actually *hit* a woman?"

"It wouldn't be the first time, M'Lord."

Lord Ravenscar sat up in bed.

He remembered that there had been blood at the

Marriage-Service, which seemed to him now to have taken place in a kind of foggy haze.

He could hear Joshua's voice intoning the words: "Wilt thou take this man to be thy lawful wedded husband?" But he could not remember what she had replied.

Then he had looked at her when the Service was over and thought that she was in fact the ugliest woman he had ever seen.

Then someone must have ceased to hold her up, because she collapsed in a crumpled heap at his feet.

'My wife!' he thought. 'My—wife!'

He wondered if there was any serious insanity in his family.

Chapter Two

Lord Ravenscar was finishing his breakfast when Viscount Garson walked into the room carrying a newspaper.

"Good-morning, Anthony!" Lord Ravenscar said.

"Here is *The Gazette*," the Viscount replied, "which all your friends will now be gaping at with protruding eyes."

Lord Ravenscar did not reply. He merely poured himself another cup of coffee.

"I presume you are still brave enough to face the gossips and ride with me in the Park?" the Viscount asked, seating himself at the table.

Lord Ravenscar's face darkened and he said curtly:

"I started this thing, and I will see it through, whatever it costs me."

"I am only sorry," the Viscount remarked, "that we cannot be present when Atalie reads the announcement of your marriage."

Again Lord Ravenscar did not reply, he merely helped himself from a dish of sweetbreads cooked with cream and mushrooms, which was offered to him by one of his flunkeys.

The Viscount glanced at him, then asked:

"She is still unconscious?"

"So I believe," Lord Ravenscar replied. "Sir William says it is a very bad case of concussion."

"It must have been caused when she hit the

pavement," the Viscount said reflectively. "The steps at Wychbold's house are quite steep, and if, as you were told, he threw her down them, it would undoubtedly have been a dangerous fall."

"Dangerous is the word," Lord Ravenscar said. "Whatever the woman may have done, Wychbold is a swine, as he always was."

"Have you learnt any more about her?" the Viscount enquired.

"I have read a letter that was in her handbag," Lord Ravenscar replied.

The Viscount looked puzzled for a moment, then he said:

"Of course, the letter which told us what her name was."

"It was written by someone called Caryl," Lord Ravenscar explained. "She begged Romara to come to her immediately. It sounded as if she was in trouble of some sort."

"She is very likely to be if Wychbold has anything to do with it," the Viscount remarked. "I suppose when the woman upstairs regains consciousness she will be able to tell us more."

"If she does, what am I supposed to do about it?" Lord Ravenscar asked.

He pushed back his plate as he spoke and rose to his feet.

"I am not blaming anyone for this," he said, "but it is a pity that we were all of us in such a state that no-one could think clearly."

"You are right! Of course you are right!" the Viscount agreed. "But I remember feeling absolutely furious that Atalie should treat you in such a scurvy manner. I always did suspect she was an adventuress."

Lord Ravenscar, who was standing with his back to the fireplace, said in surprise:

"You thought that?"

"She went out of her way to court publicity," the Viscount replied. "Granted, she was beautiful enough to deserve it. At the same time, I would not care to see my sister acclaimed as she was by all the loose-mouthed drunkards of St. James's."

"Which includes us," Lord Ravenscar said sharply, "especially me!"

"You are not the only man who has been bowled over by an 'Incomparable'," the Viscount said soothingly.

"Nor will I be the last fool to be besotted by a pretty face," Lord Ravenscar agreed bitterly.

The Viscount sighed.

"Well, if you are still determined to put Atalie in her place, we had better be on our way to the Park, where you may be quite certain everyone will want to ask you about your bride and how she has appeared in your life all of a sudden."

"I can hardly tell them the truth."

There was a raw note in Lord Ravenscar's voice. Then he thought for a moment before he said:

"I think, Anthony, the best thing would be for you and me to say that Romara is somebody I have known for a long time—a childhood sweetheart—all that sort of stuff. It will make it sound more plausible."

"I knew you would think of something intelligent," the Viscount said admiringly.

He turned towards the door. Then he stopped to say in a very different tone:

"I am sorry about this, Trent, I am really. If I had had a modicum of sense I would have stopped you, or at least insisted on waiting until the morning, when we would all have cooled down."

"Yesterday! Today! Tomorrow! I should still have wanted to teach Atalie a lesson!" Lord Ravenscar said angrily. "And if nothing else, I shall have achieved that."

"You will indeed," the Viscount agreed.

As he followed his friend across the marble Hall and out through the front door, where their horses were waiting for them, he thought that he had in fact escaped from what was undoubtedly a designing, scheming woman.

It was not because Atalie had cold-shouldered him soon after they were acquainted that he distrusted her.

It was because he was fond enough of Lord Ravenscar to wish to save him from a marriage which he knew could only be disastrous.

Love is proverbially blind, and Lord Ravenscar had not been aware of the manner in which Atalie, even after telling him she loved him, had flirted with his friends and set out to capture the heart of every man who came within her orbit.

She was the type of woman, the Viscount thought, who would never be satisfied with one man in her life, but must always be pursued by a dozen others, whoever was hurt in the process.

But to save Lord Ravenscar from Atalie had been quite a different problem from saddling him with what he had asked for—the ugliest woman in London.

Looking back, the Viscount was appalled at what had happened. Although he had racked his brains, he could see no way to extricate his friend from the predicament he was in.

He had in fact called yesterday morning, as soon as he could get to his feet, on the Honorable Joshua Meeding, to see if the ceremony which had taken place in such a crazy manner was valid.

Joshua, who had sobered up since the night before but was still somewhat aggressive, was affronted by the suggestion that he had done anything illegal.

"Naturally I have to register the marriage today," he said, "but it was perfectly legal for me to perform the ceremony and nothing but an Act of Parliament can undo it."

"Are you sure of that?" the Viscount questioned.

Not believing his friend Joshua, he had made enquiries at other sources.

Although the Act of 1754 insisted that every marriage should be registered after it took place, it was, even without registration, completely binding if performed by a Parson in Holy Orders.

"We will have to make the best of a very bad job," the Viscount told himself mournfully.

As there could be no way of keeping secret what had happened, the only possible thing to do, Lord Ravenscar decided, was to brazen it out.

This decision resulted in his sending an announcement to the *London Gazette* to state that the marriage had taken place "quietly, owing to mourning."

The explanation was by the Viscount, on the assumption that it was the truth.

He remembered noticing that Romara was wearing sombre black and the cloak and bonnet which had been carried with her handbag into the house after her were also black.

No-one, he told himself, would affect such crow-like garments unless there was a reason for it, and the fact that the marriage had been so quiet would evoke a great deal of speculation unless a plausible excuse was given for it.

He knew, however, as he and Lord Ravenscar set out towards the Park, mounted on the spirited horse-flesh which had always been the envy of their friends, that nothing could really alleviate the uncomfortable and unpleasant time that lay ahead of his friend.

* * *

Romara stirred, tried to open her eyes, and realised that one was covered with a bandage.

A woman who had been sitting by a window sewing heard the movement she made and came to the bed-side.

"Are you awake, M'Lady?" she asked. "Can you hear me?"

Through lips that seemed very stiff and painful Romara managed to say:

"Where . . . am . . . I?"

"Don't talk for a moment, M'Lady," the woman said in a quiet voice, "but try and swallow this medicine which the Physician has left for you."

She poured something from a bottle into a spoon and very carefully held it to Romara's lips.

Gentle though she was, as the spoon touched Romara's mouth it was extremely painful and she winced before she swallowed a sweet, sticky substance.

However, it immediately eased the constriction in her throat.

She looked at the woman bending over her and thought she had never seen her before.

"Where... am... I?" she managed to ask again.

"Your Ladyship's quite safe," the woman said soothingly, "and in good hands. Go to sleep, M'Lady, and I'll tell you all about it next time you wake."

The medicine Romara had drunk seemed to be very soothing and she was in fact very tired.

She had the feeling that there were a great number of problems pressing on her mind, and yet she was not sure what they were.

Obediently she closed the one eye through which she could see and fell into a dreamless slumber.

* * *

She awoke to find that it was night and the curtains were drawn, and there was a candle burning by the bed-side and by the light of it she knew she was in a room she had never seen previously.

It was very luxuriously furnished and was far more impressive than the bed-room she occupied at home.

But if she was not at home, where was she?

She realised she was not alone and saw that in an arm-chair in front of the fireplace there was a woman, not the one she had seen previously but someone younger and wearing a mob-cap of a housemaid.

She was lying back in the chair, asleep, and Romara was thankful for the moment that she did not have to speak to her.

What had happened? Why was she here? And why was one part of her face damaged?

Then slowly, almost as if her memory was coming back to her through a dark fog, she remembered....

She recalled arriving in Curzon Street, seeing Caryl, and learning that she was to have a baby.

Then she could see Sir Harvey's angry face, hear the sound of his hand as he slapped Caryl's cheek, and hear him swearing at her.

Now Romara knew why her face was bandaged. He had hit her! Incredibly, unbelievably, Sir Harvey had hit her in the face!

After that she could remember nothing. There was only darkness and an agonising pain which seemed to trail away into oblivion.

'Perhaps I am in the same house as Caryl,' Romara thought.

Although she longed to see her sister she felt a little quiver of fear in case Sir Harvey should hit her again.

Her lips were very painful and after thinking about them for some time she raised her fingers from under the bed-clothes to touch them.

She could feel that they were swollen and a place on her cheek hurt too. She found that it was covered with a plaster.

'If he has done this to me, what has he done to Caryl?' she found herself thinking in sudden terror.

She wanted to go to her sister, go to her at once to protect her, but it was impossible for her to move.

Her head too was aching almost intolerably, and she felt as if there was no life left in her body.

'I must get well quickly,' Romara thought to herself, and fell asleep.

* * *

"But I must... get up... I must!" Romara insisted.

Sir William Knighton, Lord Ravenscar's Physician, looked at her with compassion.

"It is too soon," he said. "Much too soon. You have had a bad concussion. You were unconscious for three days."

"Three days?" Romara exclaimed. "It cannot be true!"

"You hit your head on something extremely hard," he answered, "which, I understand, was the pavement."

"The pavement?" Romara was astonished and Sir William said quickly:

"Do not worry about it at the moment. Just lie

still and try to sleep. I will come again tomorrow."

He went from the room, but Romara heard him talking in a low voice outside in the corridor to the woman who she had learnt was called Mrs. Fellows.

When the latter came back into the room she came to Romara's side.

"Is there anything you require, M'Lady? Sir William suggested you should drink as much as possible and I've some fresh lemonade here beside the bed."

"That would . . . be very . . . nice," Romara managed to say.

Mrs. Fellows lifted her head with an expert hand and she sipped from the glass, thinking that her lips were not as painful as they had been the day before.

When she was laid back on the pillows she said:

"You keep calling me 'My Lady.' I am afraid there is some mistake. My name is Shaldon—Miss Romara Shaldon."

To her surprise, Mrs. Fellows hesitated. Then she said:

"His Lordship said I could tell Your Ladyship, if you asked, that you are in fact Lady Ravenscar."

Romara stared at her with her one eye in surprise, then decided that it must be a case of mistaken identity.

Whoever had brought her here must have thought she was someone else.

"My name is . . . Romara Shaldon," she reiterated, "and I have . . . never heard of . . . Lord Ravenscar."

Mrs. Fellows drew up a chair beside the bed and sat down.

"Is Your Ladyship feeling well enough to learn the truth?" she asked.

"Yes, of course," Romara said. "I am much better. In fact, I want to get up, because there is something very . . . important I have to do, but the Doctor will not let me."

"We all have to do as Sir William says, M'Lady," Mrs. Fellows replied. "He's Doctor to His Royal Highness the Prince of Wales himself! There is no Physician more experienced in the whole length and breadth of the land!"

Romara thought quickly that in that case he was doubtless going to be very expensive, but aloud she said:

"You were going to tell me the . . . truth about why I am here."

"Yes, M'Lady. You see, it's like this . . ." Mrs. Fellows began.

She explained somewhat hesitatingly how the gentlemen who had been dining with His Lordship found her lying on the pavement outside the house next door.

They had brought her in because of a wager that they would find a bride for their host, Lord Ravenscar, who had been jilted by a very beautiful young woman who was the toast of St. James's.

Mrs. Fellows was well aware that the gentlemen, headed by the Viscount Garson, were searching for the ugliest woman in London, but she did not repeat that to Romara.

She merely explained that in revenge for the manner in which he had been jilted, His Lordship had decided he would marry somebody else before Miss Bray's engagement to the Marquis of Chester could be announced.

Romara listened to her in horror.

"Are you . . . telling me," she said at length and in a very small voice, "that I am . . . really *married* to this . . . gentleman?"

"That's the truth, M'Lady."

Romara felt as if her head were whirling round, and for one moment she thought she must be delirious to imagine that such a tale could possibly be true.

But there was something convincing about the way Mrs. Fellows spoke, and she could not imagine anyone who looked so respectable inventing such a fantastic tale unless she had been instructed to do so.

"Did . . . Lord Ravenscar ask . . . you to . . . tell me this?" she enquired after a moment.

"I think perhaps His Lordship felt embarrassed at having to tell Your Ladyship himself."

Mrs. Fellows shook her head.

"His Lordship's always had a temper, although a nicer gentleman never walked the earth. But when he is in one of his rages there's no holding him!"

"One of his . . . rages?" Romara repeated faintly.

"It's in the family, M'Lady. A curse on the Ravenscars, if you like, and very angry they all gets at times. But I've never known His Lordship to do anything as wild as this before—indeed I haven't!"

"What is . . . going to . . . happen? What can I . . . do about . . . it?" Romara asked.

There was something child-like and frightened in the question, which appealed to Mrs. Fellows's maternal instinct.

"Now don't be worrying yourself, M'Lady," she said. "Things will sort themselves out when you are better, and His Lordship'll think of something, you can be sure of that!"

"You say it was a . . . real Parson who . . . married us?"

"Yes indeed, M'Lady. The Honourable Joshua Meeding was ordained several years ago, but he has no Parish and does not behave as a Parson should. Though I dare say it's presumptuous of me to say so."

It all sounded to Romara like an insane nightmare!

She could only pray that that was what it was and she would wake up to find that the whole thing was just a figment of her imagination.

Then her thoughts flew to Caryl.

What must her sister have thought when Sir Harvey, having hit her, had thrown her down the steps and onto the pavement?

She remembered now that Caryl had screamed. She had heard it quite distinctly before the pain had rendered her unconscious.

She put out her hand and held on to Mrs. Fellows.

"Do you . . . think you could . . . possibly do . . . something for . . . me?" she asked.

"You know I'll do anything in my power, M'Lady," Mrs. Fellows answered.

"Then could you find out, without anyone knowing that I have enquired, if the lady next door is well?"

"The lady next door?" Mrs. Fellows repeated.

"In Sir Harvey Wychbold's house. But no-one must be told who is asking, and above all Sir Harvey must not know that I am here."

"I'll have a word with Mr. Hignet, His Lordship's Valet, M'Lady," Mrs. Fellows promised. "He's friendly with the Butler next door and he could easily find out what Your Ladyship wishes to know."

"Then please do so . . . do so as quickly as . . . possible!" Romara begged. "I must find out how the lady is."

Mrs. Fellows brought her the information about two hours later.

Romara knew as soon as she came into the room that she had something to impart.

"Mr. Hignet's made enquiries, M'Lady," she said, "and there's no need to worry. The lady's in good health and there's no Doctor been sent for."

That was not to say that Caryl was not ill, Romara thought, remembering the way she had learnt Sir Harvey was treating her.

At the same time, she was certain that the servants would be well informed about Caryl.

If they said she was in good health, she assuredly had not made herself ill, as Romara had feared, over Sir Harvey's behaviour.

Romara felt, however, that Mrs. Fellows had more to say.

"What is it?" she asked.

"Mr. Hignet learnt that the lady's not very happy, M'Lady. She cries a lot, especially when she's alone and Sir Harvey's not in the house."

"I have to get up, whatever Sir William may say," Romara said. "If I go on lying here I shall be so weak it will take days to get me on my feet."

"Those were Sir William's instructions, M'Lady."

"I do not care!" Romara replied. "I want you to help me out of bed this afternoon, Mrs. Fellows, so that I shall be strong enough tomorrow to persuade him to let me dress and go downstairs."

Reluctantly, but because it seemed that Romara was determined, Mrs. Fellows helped her from the bed onto her feet.

Romara was surprised at how weak and feeble she felt, but she knew that if she was to help Caryl she would be unable to do so if she herself was incapacitated.

On Mrs. Fellows's arm she managed to cross the room and sit down on a chair by the window.

As she did so she caught sight of her reflection in the mirror on the dressing-table and was shocked into a horrified exclamation.

"Now, M'Lady, don't you go upsetting yourself," Mrs. Fellows admonished. "Your face's badly bruised, but Sir William says 'twas extremely fortunate that Your Ladyship's nose wasn't broken or your teeth knocked out."

"Have you a hand-mirror?" Romara asked.

"As a matter of fact there's one on the dressing-table that belonged, when she were alive, to His Lordship's mother," Mrs. Fellows replied. "As Your Ladyship had nothing with you, her things have come in useful."

For the first time Romara remembered that her trunk was next door.

"It is very kind of you," she said, "but I have a trunk of my own."

"Then I can send a carriage for it, M'Lady," Mrs. Fellows said.

Romara hesitated a moment. Then she said:

"Actually the trunk is next door, but I would not wish Sir Harvey to know where I am."

"I understand, M'Lady," Mrs. Fellows answered, "and I'm certain Mr. Hignet can arrange everything very discreetly."

"That would be very kind," Romara said.

She wondered whether she should send a note to Caryl, then thought that if it fell into Sir Harvey's hands he might treat her even more cruelly than he had done already.

She was quite certain that as he had been so

secretive about Caryl, he would not want Lord Ravenscar to know about her.

If he learnt that her sister had been taken in next door and had actually married the owner, he would inevitably work off his rage on Caryl.

'I have to save her somehow!' Romara thought.

Then as Mrs. Fellows handed her the mirror she wondered if she would ever be able to go anywhere or be seen in public again.

What she could see of her face was quite unrecognisable.

One eye was almost unaffected, but even that was slightly swollen because her usually small nose was twice its normal size and the skin nearest to the bandaged eye was bruised and turning a deep purple.

Her lips also were so swollen that they looked almost Negroid and were split in the centre.

Part of her face was obscured by the bandage and by the plaster which covered, what she saw when Mrs. Fellows dressed it, a deep gash doubtless made by a signet-ring.

"I look horrible!" Romara said in a low voice, and she could not believe it was in fact her own face.

"It'll all go, M'Lady," Mrs. Fellows replied. "It's very much better than it was and every day the swelling goes down."

Resolutely Romara put down the mirror.

It did not matter what she looked like. What was important was to help Caryl.

She hesitated a moment, then she said:

"Do you think it would be... possible for me to... speak to ... Lord Ravenscar?"

"Yes, of course, M'Lady," Mrs. Fellows said instantly. "His Lordship's been enquiring about you every day."

"Then if you will find something to put round me," Romara said, "and tidy my hair, perhaps he would speak with me for a moment."

She thought as she spoke that personally she had no wish to see Lord Ravenscar and she was quite certain he had no wish to see her.

Yet the feelings of neither of them were of consequence beside Caryl's suffering and the fact that her sister was in two months time going to have a baby without a name.

"Maybe even sooner," Romara calculated, remembering the date on which Caryl had run away with Sir Harvey.

Mrs. Fellows brought her a negligé of blue velvet trimmed with Venetian lace, which was more attractive than anything Romara had ever worn.

She covered Romara's knees with an ermine rug which she told her had belonged to the late Lady Ravenscar, then tidied what could be seen of Romara's hair under the bandage.

It was almost agonising to have her head touched because there was a very large bruise on the back of it where she had fallen on the pavement.

But Mrs. Fellows was very gentle and when she had finished she said:

"Shall I fetch His Lordship now, M'Lady? I think he's in the house."

"Please ask him to see me," Romara replied. Then she added: "But . . . could you . . . pull the . . . curtains a . . . little. The light is rather . . . bright and my eye aches."

This was really only an excuse because she was aware of how hideous she looked and feared that just as it had been a shock to her it would doubtless be a worse shock to the man to whom she was married.

Then she told herself it did not matter in the least what she looked like or what he thought.

He must be as bad a character as Sir Harvey, if not worse, to have behaved in such a disgraceful manner and to have been so drunk that he had lost all sense of decency.

Romara had, of course, heard stories of the wild gambling and hard drinking of the Bucks and Beaus and that they were encouraged by the behaviour of the Prince of Wales.

All England knew that the Prince was so drunk on his wedding-night that he had fallen into the fireplace.

All England was informed, if not by the gossips by the cartoonists, that the Prince of Wales's dearest friends drank to excess and behaved when they were drunk in an outrageous manner.

Romara had heard stories of Steeple-Chases with all the contenders wearing nightshirts, of watchmen being assaulted, of thousands of pounds being expended on ridiculous and childish wagers between men who had nothing better to do with their money than gamble it away.

However, she had never heard of anyone marrying for a wager, especially a man not in need of money.

Judging by what she had seen of the house and learnt from Mrs. Fellows of the number of servants employed, she could only imagine that Lord Ravenscar was a "Rake."

This was the type of young man which her father had always spoken of so scathingly, and perhaps he was also a libertine, as the General had thought Sir Harvey to be.

"Yet, if he has any decency in him at all," Romara told herself, "I must somehow persuade him to help Caryl. There is no-one else."

At the same time, she was terribly afraid that the man she had married would be concerned with nothing but his own pleasure.

She wondered what would happen to her, seeing the predicament into which he had brought her, but that was a problem which could be solved later.

Where Caryl was concerned the matter was urgent and thoughts of anything else must be set aside.

One thing, Romara thought, was that Lord Ravenscar was unlikely to be drunk so early in the day.

She hoped also, remembering what Mrs. Fellows had said, that he would not be in a temper.

It was easy to think things out in her brain in what she believed was a calm and sensible manner.

But her heart was beating apprehensively and her mouth felt dry and her hands were trembling when after what seemed a very long time she heard voices outside the door.

She recognized Mrs. Fellows's tone and knew that what she was saying was being answered by a man's deep voice.

Romara drew in her breath as the door opened.

"His Lordship!" Mrs. Fellows announced simply, and a man came into the room.

Romara had not really considered what Lord Ravenscar might look like except that she was sure he would be debauched, and perhaps florid and red-faced like Sir Harvey.

Worse still, he might be like the cartoons which depicted the Prince of Wales and his cronies, swollen and bloated, their cravats crumpled, their stomachs protruding.

At the first glance she saw that Lord Ravenscar was none of these things. He was tall—taller than she had expected—broad-shouldered, and undeniably handsome.

He was dressed in the height of fashion, and his high cravat, with the points of his collar showing above a square chin, was crisp and white.

There was a fob glittering beneath his waist-coat, but otherwise he was quietly if elegantly dressed, in the way ordained by Beau Brummell, which was that clothes should be part of the man and unobtrusive.

He crossed the room.

Because Romara could not at the last moment bear to see the shock in his expression or the disgust in his eyes when he looked at her, she glanced down and found it impossible to speak.

"You asked me to come and see you," Lord Ravenscar said.

"Y-yes."

It was difficult to voice such a simple word.

"I have asked daily if it would be possible to do so," he answered, "but I understand Sir William forbade it."

"I . . . had to . . . see you," Romara answered. "There is . . . something I want to . . . ask you."

"I can understand that," Lord Ravenscar replied, "and I wish, of course, to apologise."

"N-no . . . please," Romara interrupted, and held up her hand.

She felt that he was surprised, but he was silent and she said:

"I do not want to talk about myself. We can do that later. At the moment I want your . . . help, and I want it . . . urgently!"

Lord Ravenscar sat down in a chair facing Romara.

"Of course I will help you, if it is possible, he said, "but I am afraid the predicament . . ."

"It is not that," Romara interrupted again. "It concerns . . . my sister."

Lord Ravenscar raised his dark eye-brows as if he thought it curious that she should be concerned with her sister instead of herself and him.

"Your sister?" he queried.

"Yes. She is next door with Sir Harvey Wychbold."

"So it is your sister you went to see when he treated you in such an appalling manner!"

"He was . . . angry because she had . . . sent for me," Romara explained. "She had not . . . told him she had done so, and he . . . he threw me out."

"So I understand," Lord Ravenscar said dryly.

There was a note in his voice that told Romara without words how strongly he condemned Sir Harvey's behaviour.

It encouraged her to say pleadingly:

"Please . . . will you help Caryl . . . as I am unable to do so at the moment?"

"What do you suggest I do?" Lord Ravenscar asked.

"Get her away," Romara replied. "Sir Harvey is . . . ill-treating her. He hit her when I was there."

"I always knew he was an outsider!" Lord Ravenscar exclaimed. "And his behaviour towards you and what you tell me about your sister only confirms my opinion of him."

He paused. Then he asked:

"Are you quite certain that your sister wishes to leave?"

Romara twisted her fingers together as she said:

"He . . . persuaded Caryl to run . . . away with him after my father . . . forbade him to enter the house."

"He promised to marry her, I suppose?" Lord Ravenscar said.

Romara tried to nod her head, but it hurt her to do so and she winced.

"Yes, he promised her that not once but a dozen times, and Caryl was . . . in love with him."

She felt that Lord Ravenscar looked scornful and she added quickly:

"She had never seen a man like him. In fact, although she was so pretty, there were few gentlemen in Huntingdonshire to tell her so."

"So Wychbold swept her off her feet," Lord Ravenscar said contemptuously. "I am sure this is not the first time he has behaved in such a manner."

"I was sure, although my father forbade me to communicate with her, that Sir Harvey had married Caryl," Romara said.

"You could hardly expect a bounder of that description to keep his word," Lord Ravenscar replied. "But if your sister wishes to leave him, why does she not do so?"

"He keeps her virtually prisoner in the house," Romara answered, "and . . ."

There was silence for a moment and Lord Ravenscar saw the colour rising crimson on the one side of her face that was visible.

"And . . . she is having a . . . baby!" Romara finished in a very low voice.

"I suppose I might have expected that."

There was something cynical in the way he spoke, which made Romara feel despairingly that he was not going to interfere.

"Please . . . please help her," she begged. "I have . . . . no-one else to ask. My father would have dealt with Sir Harvey very effectively, but he is dead."

"It seems a strange question to have to ask," Lord Ravenscar said, "but would you tell me who you are and who your father was?"

"My father was General Sir Alexander Shaldon," Romara said, and realised that Lord Ravenscar was staring at her in astonishment.

"Your father commanded the Tenth Light Dragoon Guards?"

"Yes."

"Good Heavens! I served under him!" Lord Ravenscar exclaimed. "But how in the name of Heaven could the General have allowed a man like Wychbold to come into contact with your sister or you?"

"Sir Harvey was introduced to Caryl by a neighbour, and when he called to see her, and sent her flowers and wrote her love-letters, Papa forbade him to come to the house."

"So I should think," Lord Ravenscar remarked.

"But Sir Harvey persuaded Caryl to go on seeing him secretly."

"I am sure he was very persuasive." Lord Ravenscar's voice was sarcastic.

"Please understand," Romara pleaded, "Caryl had never met anyone like him. I think he mesmerised her."

"And now she is having his child. God knows what your father would think about it if he were alive."

"I think Papa would have killed Sir Harvey, or else made him marry Caryl to give the child a name," Romara said.

Lord Ravenscar looked at her in a startled fashion.

"Is that what she wants?"

"I think she is too upset and distressed to know what she wants," Romara answered. "I only saw her for a few moments, but she told me that Sir Harvey is . . . angry with her for having a baby and is trying to keep the . . . knowledge of it hidden."

"That does not surprise me."

"Caryl thinks too," Romara went on in a very small voice, "that Sir Harvey is . . . bored with her and . . . interested in another . . . woman."

She saw Lord Ravenscar's mouth tighten. Then he said aloud:

"Will you leave this problem with me? I want to discuss it with a friend of mine, but I promise you one thing, I will do something about it."

"And soon?" Romara asked anxiously.

"As quickly as possible," Lord Ravenscar promised.

"I am so afraid he may be treating her as he treated me," Romara said.

"You certainly owe him something for that. What had you done to incense him?"

"I only told him what I thought of him."

Lord Ravenscar laughed.

"As your father's daughter, it is rather what I would have expected you to do, but perhaps it was unwise in the circumstances."

"He . . . hit Caryl for asking me to . . . come to her," Romara said. "Then he . . . hit me."

She drew in her breath at the memory of it.

"I do not remember anything after that."

"That is what I suspected," Lord Ravenscar said, "but I gather Mrs. Fellows had told you what in fact had occurred."

"Yes."

"As you suggested," he said quickly, "we will discuss that later. I do see that your sister's predicament at the moment is more important than anything else."

"Thank . . . you. Thank you for . . . saying you will . . . try to . . . help her," Romara said.

"When is the baby due?"

Again the colour came into Romara's face.

It seemed so improper, almost indecent, to be discussing an unborn baby with a strange man.

Then she told herself severely that this was not the moment for girlish modesty or shyness.

"Caryl thinks in . . . two months," she answered, "but it may be . . . sooner."

"Then we certainly have to act quickly," Lord Ravenscar said. "You are quite certain it would be in your sister's best interests to marry this swine?"

Romara made a little gesture with her hands.

"Whatever he is like, he is still the father of the

child. How could she bear the . . . stigma of . . . having it and being . . . unmarried?"

She paused before she said in a worried voice:

"If I take her home—supposing Sir Harvey allowed me to—we would have to make some explanation to our neighbours."

"I can understand that."

Lord Ravenscar looked at Romara and she thought that he looked away quickly because he could not bear the sight of her face.

"Leave everything to me," he said. "I promise you I will give this a great deal of thought and try to come up with a solution."

"Thank you. It is very, very kind of you. I was afraid you would not understand how important it is."

"I do understand," he answered, "and perhaps that is one good point in my favour. I cannot expect you to find many."

He smiled at her a little wryly. Then he walked towards the door.

"Hurry up and get well," he said in a surprisingly kind voice. "I have a feeling that you are going to need all your strength!"

Chapter Three

Sir Harvey Wychbold, driving beside Lord Windover, who was tooling a magnificent pair of bays, had a smile of satisfaction on his face.

He could hardly believe his good fortune when the previous evening at Wattiers, Lord Windover, who was standing next to him at the Bar, discussed a Mill that was to take place at Wimbledon and suggested they should watch it together.

Ever since he had come to London, Sir Harvey had aspired to become a social figure, but the members of the real *Beau Ton* avoided him and he had almost despaired of attaining his ambition.

It was true that because he was wealthy it was easy to ingratiate himself with the penniless members of the nobility and those who had lost their fortunes at cards, but that was not what Sir Harvey wanted.

He had been brought up in Yorkshire, and his father, an impecunious Baronet who had sold his title and himself to the daughter of a rich wool manufacturer, had refused to allow him to leave home.

It was a disastrous decision, because Harvey Wychbold, with nothing else to occupy his mind, had seduced every attractive woman within thirty miles of his home.

He longed with an unabated intensity for wider fields in which to exploit his own particular talents.

As soon as his father had died he left Yorkshire,

ready to enjoy the life of gaiety and frivolity in London, of which he had heard so many stories.

By this time the new Baronet had reached the age of thirty and was well aware of his attractions where women were concerned.

He had not calculated, however, that the gentlemen whom he sought to make his friends should "cold-shoulder" him.

His first set-back came when he found he was blackballed from White's Club and also from Brooks's.

He did not know who his enemies were but it was evident that he had them, and although again every year he tried to become a member of the two most exclusive Clubs in St. James's, his name was invariably turned down.

He did, however, manage to belong to two minor Clubs, and of course places like Wattiers and the other gambling "halls" were only too eager to welcome him.

Then last year he had visited Huntingdonshire and stayed with a riotous party in the house of a young Nobleman who had borrowed quite a considerable sum from him over the years.

It was so enjoyable that Sir Harvey began to think his ambitions might be more easily gratified if he approached them from a different angle.

He had in fact been genuinely captivated by the youth, freshness, and charm of Caryl, but what had been equally important in his mind was her background.

He did not miss how General Sir Alexander Shaldon was spoken of with great respect and that it was obvious he was a welcome guest in any house in the County he cared to visit.

Sir Harvey had set siege to Caryl's heart with a confidence that was characteristic.

He was an extremely conceited man, and there was no doubt in his mind that sooner or later, however difficult it might appear, he would become one of the intimates of the Prince of Wales's set.

When the General forbade him to visit the house he was surprised, but he was quite certain that the old man doted on his two daughters and would undoubtedly change his mind.

He persuaded Caryl to run away with him and was astounded when after they reached London her letters to her father were returned unopened and there were no communications from her sister.

It was then that Sir Harvey realised he had made a mistake, and it was brought home to him even more forcefully when he found that Caryl was having a baby.

The last thing he wanted was to be saddled with a wife who had no importance in the Social World and a baby whose grandfather would not acknowledge it.

What was more, Sir Harvey's affection for Caryl, if that was the right word for it, was on the wane.

He had met a widow who, too late he had thought, would have made a better wife from a social point of view than anyone else with whom he had come in contact.

"But is it too late?" he began to ask himself, and started to search for a way in which he could be rid of Caryl.

The whole problem was tiresomely difficult and worrying. However, the evening of Romara's arrival in answer to Caryl's plea for help had brought Sir Harvey a devastating blow.

While he was quite confident that the widow was his for the asking, he delayed too long in assuring her that his interest in her was strictly honourable.

After an intimate dinner she told him quietly but firmly that she intended to marry somebody else.

Inevitably and unfortunately, Sir Harvey put the blame for his losing the widow entirely on Caryl.

If Caryl had not been living in his house, he told himself, he would have proposed marriage far sooner.

He had gone home in a rage that had not been lessened by the amount of brandy he had drunk after his proposal had been refused.

He had hit Caryl, as he had often done before, but he had certainly not intended to strike her sister.

The mere fact that Romara was present, and that

Caryl had sent for her behind his back, made him so furious that he lost control of his actions.

The following morning he wondered apprehensively if Romara would make trouble, but the day passed without incident and he told himself with characteristic cock-sureness that she would have returned to the country.

He was only one of the many people who, the following day, were astounded to read in *The Gazette* that Lord Ravenscar had married Romara Shaldon.

At first Sir Harvey could not believe it. It seemed impossible that he should have done so. Then he thought it might have been the reason why Romara had called on Caryl.

Because he had no wish for there to be further trouble, he hid *The Gazette* so that Caryl should not see it, and gave strict instructions that no-one, above all no-one who lived next door, should be admitted into the house.

What Sir Harvey did not know, and which would have infuriated him if he had, was that his servants had already been bribed to take Romara's trunk next door.

Sir Harvey, like many rich men, was not a kindly or a generous master.

He sacked his servants for minor offences, paid them a minimum wage, and was extremely cheese-paring when it came to providing food for the Servants' Hall.

It was his grandfather's Yorkshire strain coming out in him, and the servants reacted in an understandable manner in that they gave him lip-service but did not consider he had earned their loyalty.

Notes passed backwards and forwards between the two houses, of which Sir Harvey had no knowledge, and the fact that those leaving Lord Ravenscar's house were invariably accompanied by a golden sovereign made the transference easy and secret.

Somehow, Sir Harvey knew, he had to extricate himself from what he thought of as "the clutches of

Caryl," but for the moment an acceptable way of doing so escaped him.

Now, however, driving towards Wimbledon, he put Caryl out of his mind and concentrated on making himself fulsomely pleasant to Lord Windover.

A quiet man, Lord Windover's one pleasure when he was in London was gaming.

He was always welcome at Carlton House and the Prince of Wales had often stayed at Windover Park in Berkshire.

The conversation on the way to Wimbledon was mostly about the Mill which the two gentlemen were to watch.

Bombardier Tom Bard, the protégé of the Viscount Garson, was to be matched against Jeb Salt, the local champion.

"Personally, I favour Bard," Lord Windover said. "Garson is a good judge of a pugilist and I always suspect that local champions get too sure of themselves."

"I am sure you are right about that," Sir Harvey replied, "and I shall definitely put my money on Bard."

They reached the place on Wimbledon Common where the fight was to take place, to find that the usual farm-carts and bales of hay had been arranged for the spectators.

There was a number of the Viscount's friends, all extremely elegant, wagering large sums of money on Bard, while the local Gentry and spectators from the neighbourhood were backing Salt.

Lord Windover handed the reins to his groom and he and Sir Harvey joined the other gentlemen who were sitting on the hay-bales closest to the Ring.

The fight began almost as soon as they arrived, and there was no doubt, despite Lord Windover's confidence in him, that the Bombardier would not have an easy victory.

It was in consequence an excellent fight, and it was only after an hour had passed that the Bombardier, bleeding profusely and starting to sag at the knees, finally knocked down Jeb Salt.

"A fine fight! Outstanding!" everyone exclaimed.

The Viscount handed his protégé a purse of gold, while Jeb Salt, although he was the loser, received some compensation for having put up such a good show.

"I congratulate you, Garson!" Lord Windover said.

"Thank you," the Viscount replied. "And we must certainly celebrate. Will you dine with me tonight? I am giving a small party."

"I will be delighted!" Lord Windover replied.

Then to Sir Harvey's astonishment and satisfaction the Viscount said carelessly:

"Will you join us, Wychbold—if you have no prior engagement?"

"I should be honoured!" Sir Harvey said quickly.

He knew that no previous engagement could be important enough to prevent him from accepting such an invitation.

Never before had the Viscount or any of his friends behaved as if they were even aware of his existence.

Yet now he had been asked to a dinner which, he told himself excitedly, might prove to be a turning point in his life.

"Where are we to dine?" Lord Windover asked.

"In the family mausoleum in Park Lane. My father is in the country and I have the house to myself."

"At seven-thirty, I suppose?" Lord Windover asked.

"Yes, at seven-thirty," the Viscount answered, "and do not be late. Brummell is coming and he dislikes waiting for his food."

Listening, Sir Harvey could hardly believe his ears.

It was a triumph that he should be asked by the Viscount to an intimate dinner with his friends.

But that Beau Brummell should be one of the guests made him feel that at last his goal, which had seemed so elusive, was not only in sight but he had actually reached it!

Beau Brummell had made himself not only the Arbiter of Fashion but also the most important personality in the whole of the *Beau Monde*.

The success or failure of any party depended largely upon whether he was present.

That he was so closely associated with the Prince of Wales, who visited him every morning to hear him gossip and watch him dress, was observed with envy, jealousy, and malice by those who disliked Brummell's arrogance.

Yet there was no doubt that he occupied a unique place in the Social World, from which it would be very hard to dislodge him.

All Sir Harvey had ever longed for was to meet Beau Brummell and to be able to boast of it afterwards.

He had seen him, of course, often enough, and it was impossible not to admire a man who expressed in himself all the rules and regulations he had laid down for others to follow.

Sir Harvey had never forgotten a letter his mother had received from a friend when George Brummell had first appeared in the Social Sphere.

The lady had written:

> *Nature has been most liberal to this charming man. He is about the same height as Apollo and the just proportions of his form are remarkable! His head is particularly well shaped, his face rather long, his complexion fair, his forehead unusually high.*
>
> *His countenance indicates that he possesses considerable intelligence and his mouth betrays a strong disposition to indulge his sardonic humour. His voice is very pleasing.*

Lady Wychbold's correspondent had not exaggerated all that was true of Beau Brummell, and many people found him good-humoured and kind.

It was known that he could, if he wished, be unswervingly loyal to those he called his friends.

Sir Harvey was not really interested in Beau

Brummell's disposition except in how it could concern himself.

He longed to know him; he had prayed to make his acquaintance; and now the opportunity had quite unexpectedly presented itself.

By the time they had driven back to London it was obvious that Lord Windover and Sir Harvey would have to hurry if they were to be on time for the dinner at the Viscount's house.

"I will pick you up," Lord Windover said as he dropped Sir Harvey in Curzon Street.

Another favour!

For Lord Windover was certainly aware that Sir Harvey had his own horses.

As soon as he was inside his own front door Sir Harvey shouted to his Valet and hurried up the stairs, cursing the man for not joining him as quickly as he wished.

He was in a considerable flutter as to what he should wear.

Fortunately he had spent a fortune on his clothes, and as the Valet always had everything pressed and ready it was only a question of which long-tailed coat fitted him the more closely, and in which style his muslin cravat should be tied.

Sir Harvey remembered that Beau Brummell had set his face against the vulgar ostentations of the Marcaronis, the affectations of the Whigs, and the boorishness of the Bucks.

He stood simply for moderate good taste and he had said:

"The severest mortification a gentleman could incur would be to attract observation in the street by his outward appearance."

Sir Harvey's Valet broke in on his thoughts.

"Will you be wearing a tie-pin, Sir?"

"No, of course not, you fool! Brummell is to be one of the guests."

Sir Harvey could not help boasting even to his Valet about whom he would meet.

"Then you'll not need your fob, Sir."

"Certainly not!" Sir Harvey snapped, pulling off

the signet-ring he habitually wore on one of his fingers as he spoke.

When he was dressed he surveyed himself with satisfaction. His cravat was a model of crispness and was tied in a style that Beau Brummell himself had initiated.

His silk stockings fitted without a wrinkle, and his coat had been cut by Schweitzer, the tailor that the Beau and the Prince of Wales patronised.

"You look exceedingly smart, Sir!" the Valet said with just the right note of flattery in his voice.

Sir Harvey smiled at his own reflection in the mirror.

"I will order another coat tomorrow," he said. "Schweitzer has done me well, and he shall have the privilege of making it."

"I'm sure he'll be very gratified, Sir," the Valet murmured.

Sir Harvey gave a sigh of satisfaction.

After tonight he envisaged many evenings when he would be dining with the *Ton*.

Already he was rehearsing in his mind the amusing anecdotes he would relate, a witty turn of phrase which might gain the approval even of Brummell himself.

At exactly five-and-twenty past seven Lord Windover's London Cabriolet drew up outside the door and it was with difficulty that Sir Harvey restrained himself from hurrying down the steps before the bell was rung.

As he joined Lord Windover in the carriage he said:

"I am looking forward to this evening. I have not seen Garson's family house. I thought he had lodgings of his own."

"He has, when his father, the Earl, is in residence," Lord Windover replied, "but actually the old man seldom comes to London these days. He is in ill-health, I believe."

"And of course a large house makes entertaining much easier," Sir Harvey remarked.

He decided at that moment that Curzon Street

was not big enough for him. He would move to Berkeley Square, or perhaps Park Lane—why not? He had plenty of money!

With a quickening pulse he visualised giving dinner-parties with his new friends, and, although perhaps it was too much to hope, Beau Brummell might be among them.

It was only a short drive to where a large and impressive Mansion owned by the Viscount's father stood back from Park Lane, surrounded by its own garden.

As Lord Windover entered through the front door, Sir Harvey, following him, was taking notes on how his new house would be furnished.

He was aware that there were no less than six footmen in attendance, besides a Butler, and their liveries were considerably more impressive than those of his own footmen.

'There are a great many things I shall have to alter,' he thought to himself.

Then the Butler in stentorian tones was announcing them: "Lord Windover—Sir Harvey Wychbold!"

There were about fourteen men in the room already. As they all seemed to turn their heads in his direction, Sir Harvey thought with satisfaction that he recognised a number of them.

Lord Charles Manners and his brother, Lord Robert Manners, sons of the Duke of Rutland, were the first two he spotted.

Then he found it hard to look further than Beau Brummell.

He appeared, Sir Harvey thought, somewhat aloof and disdainful, but that was almost an habitual expression.

He was however paying attention to what was being said by an older man who had the appearance and bearing of a soldier.

Lord Windover moved across the room to where almost at the far end of it their host was standing.

The Viscount did not shake hands with him but merely said:

"Now that you have arrived, Windover, I think we can start the proceedings."

As he spoke he held up his hand, and as if at a signal everyone present fell silent.

"I have asked you here tonight," the Viscount said in a loud, clear voice, "because we all, with one exception, have something in common. It is, as you well know, that we have all served at one time or another in the Tenth Light Dragoon Guards and came under the command of General Sir Alexander Shaldon."

With a little murmur from those listening, the Viscount continued:

"He was a great man and a just man, and although we often had reason to fear him, I think in our hearts we always respected and admired him."

Again there was a murmur of approval.

"That is why," the Viscount went on, "I felt you would like to be present tonight to witness the marriage between the General's daughter, Miss Caryl Shaldon, and Sir Harvey Wychbold!"

Sir Harvey gave an audible gasp, then felt as if he were paralysed into immobility.

The eyes of every man in the room were on him and for a moment he felt that he could not have heard what had been said and there must be some mistake.

Then he knew that he had been completely and very cleverly tricked and there was nothing—nothing at all—that he could do about it!

He hardly had time to think before another door of the room opened and Caryl came in on the arm of Lord Ravenscar.

She was wearing a long white lace veil which did not cover her face but fell from her head to the floor, covering the gown, and she carried a large bouquet of white flowers which disguised her figure.

Her eyes were downcast, her lashes dark against her pale cheeks.

She looked lovely with her fair hair showing beneath an orange-blossom wreath, and the only sign she gave of being nervous was that her hand was tightly gripping Lord Ravenscar's arm.

They moved towards the Viscount, and because Sir Harvey had been beside him as he spoke he was automatically in the right place.

Then from behind the bride and her escort came a Parson in a white surplice, his medals showing that he was the Chaplain of the Regiment.

The Viscount stepped to one side and there was an absolute silence which to Sir Harvey seemed ominous and menacing.

Then the Service began, and there was nothing he could do but accept the inevitable.

He felt his heart pounding with fury in his breast and thought there was a red haze in front of his eyes.

It was a sense of self-preservation rather than pride that made him speak the words that were required of him firmly and without stumbling.

Caryl's voice was low and tremulous.

A ring appeared seemingly from nowhere and Sir Harvey placed it on her finger, their hands were joined together by the Chaplain, and the final words of the Marriage-Service were spoken.

As soon as the Chaplain's voice died away Lord Ravenscar offered Caryl his arm and once again she held on to him tightly as he drew her back towards the door through which they had entered.

As they vanished, Sir Harvey looked round and found the dinner guests formed up in two ranks, leaving a narrow passageway between.

There was no need for anyone to speak. The intention was plain and he knew what was required of him.

With his head held high, looking neither to right nor to left, he walked the length of the room and out through the door.

In the Hall the Butler handed him his hat, a footman put his cloak over his shoulders, and another flunkey was waiting to hand him into a Hackney carriage.

This was the final insult, and as Sir Harvey drove away he knew that he was not only defeated but that his grandiose ambitions of becoming a social figure had been buried so deeply that they could never be resuscitated.

* * *

In the room next to where she had been married, Caryl sank down on a chair and covered her face with her hands.

Romara put her arms round her.

"It is all right, dearest. It is all over!" she said. "You are married, but you need never see him again!"

"He will—never forgive—me," Caryl said falteringly.

"As I will never forgive him!" Romara said firmly.

Lord Ravenscar was standing near them with a glass of champagne in his hand.

"I think she ought to have a drink before you take her home," he said to Romara.

She took the glass from him and raised it to Caryl's lips.

"No! It reminds me—of him!"

"It will make you feel better," Romara said. "Have a few sips and when we get back you can have something to eat."

Caryl shook her head. Then in a voice tremulous with fear she asked:

"Wh-where are you—taking me?"

"You are coming with me to Lord Ravenscar's house," Romara replied.

"It is—next door to his," Caryl whispered. "Supposing Harvey—sees me? He might—beat me for what I have done to him."

"It is only for tonight," Lord Ravenscar interposed. "Tomorrow I am taking you and your sister to my house in the country. You will be safe there, I promise you."

It seemed as if his deep voice and his calm way of speaking reached Caryl to sweep away for the moment some of her fear.

"That will be—nice," she managed to say, and Romara drew her to her feet.

With her sister on one side of her and Lord Ravenscar on the other, Caryl walked from the room and down a passage which took them to a different door from the one by which Sir Harvey had left.

There was a closed carriage waiting, and after Caryl and Romara were safely inside Lord Ravenscar stood for a moment watching it drive away.

Then he put his hand up to his forehead.

He was more relieved than he was prepared to admit even to himself that everything had gone according to plan.

He had thought it out with Anthony Garson down to the minutest detail.

There had always been a chance that Sir Harvey would categorically refuse to marry Caryl, or that by some unforeseen chance he would not be able to accept the invitation to dinner.

Now, Lord Ravenscar thought, at any rate one problem was solved. Caryl's child would be born with a name and Wychbold had got his just deserts.

That left, he thought as he walked back along the corridor, his own difficulties to be faced.

He had found it hard to look at the woman who was now his wife, and it was still impossible to see much of her face.

He had an idea that Romara kept the bandage on because she could not bear anyone to see the deep purple and yellow bruises which surrounded her eye.

The scar on her mouth was nearly healed and her lips were no longer swollen. But she had kept her head bent and Lord Ravenscar knew that he had in fact no idea what she really looked like.

He could only hope that by some good fortune she would be as pretty as her sister must have been before she had been changed to a nervous wreck by the cruel and despicable behaviour of Wychbold.

There was only one small atom of consolation, Lord Ravenscar thought as he reached the end of the passage and heard the noise and laughter of the Viscount's guests—Romara had an attractive voice.

He had always disliked women with harsh, hard, or high voices, and Romara spoke in a voice that had something musical about it. There was no doubt that she addressed her sister with love and sympathy when she spoke to her.

'I suppose I can always shut my eyes and listen to her,' Lord Ravenscar thought grimly.

Then he opened the door and joined his friends.

* * *

Back at Curzon Street, Mrs. Fellows helped Caryl upstairs and took her into the next room to Romara's.

"I have your bed all ready, M'Lady," she said. "What you need is a good night's sleep, and everything'll seem better in the morning."

Caryl had been crying all the way back in the carriage and now she was too miserable and exhausted to reply.

"It is all right, dearest, everything is all right now," Romara said. "I am going to look after you and we will have a happy time together."

She wondered as she spoke if this was the truth—for she had not discussed it with Lord Ravenscar.

He might not want Caryl permanently with them, although she was quite certain he would not want to be alone with his wife.

She had to admit, however, that he had been exceedingly kind.

When he had told her at the last moment what was planned and how they would collect Caryl from the house next door the very moment the carriage carrying Sir Harvey was out of sight, she had exclaimed:

"How clever of you! How could you think of anything so brilliant?"

She realised that in the circumstances it would be almost impossible for Sir Harvey to make a scene which would undoubtedly prostrate Caryl and perhaps make her decide that she would not marry a man who was so reluctant.

"All you have to do," Lord Ravenscar had explained, "is to dress your sister so that she looks as attractive as possible. She naturally will not want those present to know of her condition."

Romara blushed. Then she said in a very small voice:

"I... I need not... meet anyone... need I? It would be embarrassing... both for you and for... me."

"You must do as you wish," he said. "It will be quite easy for you to stay with Caryl until the last moment, and I will take her into the room where the Viscount will be waiting."

"Thank you," Romara said, "and thank you for everything... from the very bottom of my... heart."

There was a hint of tears behind the sincerity in her voice and Lord Ravenscar said quickly:

"I am quite truthful in saying that I would not wish a daughter of my old Commanding Officer to be treated in such a scurvy manner. We are all of us exceedingly proud of having served in such a distinguished Regiment."

"I know that Papa if he were alive would be grateful too," Romara said in a low voice. "Although he would have hated having such a man as his son-in-law, Papa was very practical. He would have realised that now it is in Caryl's best interests to be married to Sir Harvey."

"I am sure that is right," Lord Ravenscar answered. "And tomorrow I will take you both to my country house and arrange for your sister to have her child there."

There was nothing Romara could do but thank him over and over again. Then her mind was busy with arrangements for Caryl's wedding-garments to be smuggled into the house next door.

Caryl's lady's-maid had by this time been well bribed into doing anything that was required of her.

Besides, Romara was certain that the woman was genuinely fond of her mistress.

As soon as Sir Harvey drove away with Lord Windover, Lord Ravenscar and Romara, who were waiting in a carriage a little way down the street, drove up to Sir Harvey's front door.

Caryl was assisted down the steps and into the carriage beside them.

She gave a little cry of happiness at seeing her sister, then looked apprehensively at Lord Ravenscar.

"It is all right," he said reassuringly. "Everything is arranged and there will be no difficulties."

"How—can you be—sure?" Caryl asked. "Harvey had gone to a—very grand—dinner-party. My maid told me that—Mr. Brummell is to be there."

"Mr. Brummell served in your father's Regiment for two years," Lord Ravenscar replied. "He was only sixteen when he received a Coronetcy from the Prince of Wales."

"I had no idea," Caryl murmured.

"What I want you to do," Lord Ravenscar said as they neared the Viscount's house, "is just to hold on to me and not be frightened."

"I will—try not to be," Caryl promised.

But when she could hear the voices of the gentlemen talking in the next room she looked so pale that Romara was afraid she might faint.

At the same time, she was aware that because Caryl reacted better to men than she did to women, Lord Ravenscar was a tower of strength to her.

"Now then," he said as the door in front of them opened, "think of your father and imagine that you are going into battle beside him."

His words seemed to rally Caryl as nothing else could have done, Romara thought.

But the effort had been too much for her, and now in bed she just sobbed helplessly against the pillows.

Mrs. Fellows drew Romara to one side.

"I'll bring Her Ladyship a glass of warm milk with calamine flowers in it to make her sleep," she said in a low voice. "It's bad for her condition to get in such a state."

Romara nodded, and a little while later, having drunk the milk, Caryl was fast asleep.

She sat beside the bed until she was certain there was no chance of her sister waking until the morning, then she went to her own bed-room.

She longed to know what had happened after they had left and what Sir Harvey had said.

Had he blustered and sworn at those who had tricked him into marriage? Or had he just remained silent?

Lord Ravenscar had gone back to the party, and although she knew that such an idea was completely impossible, she wished that she could sit up and wait for him to come home.

She could imagine that he would be horrified at the idea! The last thing he wanted was a wife and worst of all the type of wife who waited up and wanted to talk when he was tired!

As Romara undressed she wondered desperately what would happen both to her and Caryl.

How could she have ever imagined that such terrible and dramatic events would alter their lives so completely and unexpectedly?

She looked in the mirror, inspecting the dark purple and orange patch which covered her eye and half her cheek!

She felt quite certain that with his talent for organisation and imaginative planning, Lord Ravenscar was already engaged in thinking of how he could be rid of her!

* * *

It was going to be a very hot, sunny day, but they left early in the morning, both Caryl and Romara hoping that Sir Harvey would be asleep and unaware of what was happening next door.

Lord Ravenscar had suggested that they should travel in his largest Chaise as it would not only ensure that the journey took less time but would also, he thought, be less bumpy for Caryl than a carriage would have been.

A landau was to follow, carrying Mrs. Fellows, who was to go to the country with them, His Lordship's Valet, and their luggage.

Again, a number of gold sovereigns had ensured that all Caryl's clothes had been packed and brought next door, and they were now piled on the landau.

A good night's sleep seemed to have revived her

and she looked extremely pretty in a high-brimmed bonnet which tied under her chin with blue ribbons.

Romara would have had nothing to wear but the dismal black bonnet in which she had come to London, but Caryl had insisted that one of her hat-boxes should be opened.

A bonnet was found for Romara, over which she draped a lace veil which hid her face.

"You do not want to wear that tiresome bandage," Caryl said as they were dressing. "It makes you look so sinister. Put plenty of powder over the bruise, and if you wear a veil no-one will be able to see what is beneath it."

Romara had known that her sister was speaking sensibly.

Although she thought it was wrong to leave off so soon the mourning she was wearing for her father, she thought that anything that depressed Caryl should be avoided.

"One good thing," Caryl went on quite cheerfully, "is that you can wear all the clothes Harvey bought before—he became so unkind and—b-bored with me."

Romara felt it was a step in the right direction that Caryl could talk about him without crying, and she replied:

"I am very grateful, dearest. I only brought black with me from home, and to send back for my coloured gowns might cause a lot of comment."

"Of course it would!" Caryl agreed. "And the things I now possess are far more expensive than anything we have ever worn before."

She gave a little sigh before she added:

"I think at first Harvey wanted to—show off. He liked even strangers to see that he was with a—pretty woman."

Romara was sure that this was the truth, for she could not imagine Sir Harvey wishing unselfishly to please Caryl. There would have to be a personal motive behind his generosity.

Though she still had to hide her face, Romara felt a little more confident of herself than if she had been wearing the hot and uncomfortable bandage.

At the same time, she was well aware that she looked terribly unsightly and she had no wish for Lord Ravenscar to look at her closely.

Not that he seemed inclined to do so, and she was certain that he was almost as embarrassed about her appearance as she was.

It was therefore with a sense of relief as they were driving out of London that they heard Lord Ravenscar say:

"When I have installed you at Raven House I hope you will understand if I return straightaway to London. I have a long-standing engagement to attend a political dinner which the Prince is giving at Carlton House, and I think he would be extremely annoyed if I chucked him at the last moment."

"I do not wish to be a—nuisance in any way," Caryl said, while Romara replied:

"Of course you must go! I see even the newspapers are saying what a good thing it is that the Prince is taking a real interest in politics."

"His Royal Highness is delighted that his friends have come into power," Lord Ravenscar replied, "and he is in fact becoming politically influential."

"Is it true," Romara asked, "that the new Government is known as 'the Ministry of All Talents'?"

"That is how they like to think of themselves," Lord Ravenscar replied with a smile, "but you are well aware that they will have to prove it to the country."

He was in fact, as a friend of the Prince, very confident that things would improve not only politically but also for the Prince himself.

His Royal Highness had for a long period been exceedingly unpopular and misunderstood.

Now he had a chance of proving how very able and intelligent he was and, in the words of Thomas Chevening, who considered himself at the head of the Whig Party, of "being a great politician."

Romara, who had always been interested in politics, thought of a dozen questions she would have liked to ask Lord Ravenscar, but she thought he might consider it a bore.

Anyway, her father had always said: "Gentlemen dislike talking when they are driving," and so she lapsed into silence.

At the same time, she enjoyed the speed at which they were travelling, the magnificence of Lord Ravenscar's team of well-matched chestnuts, and the undulating beauty of the countryside.

Huntingdonshire, where they had lived all their lives, was flat and rather dull, but in Buckinghamshire, where Lord Ravenscar's house was situated, there were woods, hills, rivers, and fields of golden corn.

When they reached Raven House and drove down the long drive, Romara was looking eagerly through her veil to see what sort of country home Lord Ravenscar owned.

With its huge porticoed front and elegant winged sides, it was even more beautiful than she had expected, and its background of green trees and a lake in front made it exactly, she thought, the sort of country house she had always dreamt about.

As they drew nearer, a flight of white doves passed in front of them to settle on the velvety green lawns sloping down to the lake, and the sunshine glinting on the bay windows made them appear warm and welcoming.

There were a number of footmen to help them out of the Chaise and as they stepped into the Hall a Major Domo in magnificent livery came forward to say:

"Welcome back, M'Lord, and may I on behalf of the staff congratulate Your Lordship on your marriage and extend to you and Her Ladyship our warmest wishes for your happiness."

"Thank you, Matthews," Lord Ravenscar said. "As I sent a groom ahead to tell you, Her Ladyship's sister, Lady Wychbold, is in ill-health, and I think she would like to go immediately to her bed-room."

"Of course, M'Lord. And luncheon is ready whenever Your Lordship wishes."

Romara was glad that Lord Ravenscar had realised that Caryl was in a weak state and had been silent for quite a long time.

She had not slept, but her eyes had been closed and the gaiety with which she had spoken on the first part of the journey had vanished.

Now she did in fact look very ill.

A Housekeeper appeared to assist Romara to half-carry Caryl up the wide, beautifully carved staircase.

Romara was thankful that their bed-rooms were on the first floor.

She found that while she was to sleep in a large State-Room which had been used by the Chatelaines of the house for several centuries, Caryl was next door.

The first thing was to get her sister into bed. Only as they finished doing so did Caryl say weakly:

"I have—a—pain!"

Romara looked questioningly at Mrs. Fellows, who by now had joined them, and she said quietly:

"I think, M'Lady, we should send for a Doctor."

"Then would you ask His Lordship to do so?" Romara replied.

She knew it should be her task, but somehow she could not face Lord Ravenscar.

In the first place, she did not wish him to see her face, and secondly she felt embarrassed to be asking him to do more for them than he had done already.

Only a little while later they were all aware that Caryl's baby was about to be born.

Chapter Four

"Will you dine with me tomorrow evening, Trent?" the Viscount enquired.

"I think tomorrow I ought to go down to Raven House," Lord Ravenscar replied. "I have not been there for three weeks and the Prince will be away for the next few days."

"Then I think your duty obviously lies in the country," the Viscount remarked with a smile.

As if he realised that his friend did not wish to discuss the matter further, he then talked of other things.

It had in fact been pricking Lord Ravenscar's conscience that, having left Raven House when Caryl was in the throes of having her baby, he had found a dozen valid excuses for not returning there.

He had learnt from his Agent, Mr. Arkwright, who kept him in continual touch with what was happening in the country, that Caryl had produced a son.

He wondered if Sir Harvey would be interested in knowing he had an heir, but he did not intend personally to inform him of the event, although he was quite certain he would learn of it in one way or another.

What of course was important from Caryl's point of view was that the Social World should not learn she had produced a child so soon after she was married.

To make quite certain that her legal status was

recognised, Lord Ravenscar had himself sent to the *London Gazette* the announcement that the marriage had taken place.

After that he had metaphorically washed his hands of Sir Harvey and hoped he would never come in contact with him again.

He was, as it happened, extremely busy with the Prince, who, having complained that he had been insufficiently consulted about the Ministerial appointments in the new Government, was finding that with so many of his friends in Office his influence was considerable.

He wished to know everything and anything that took place in the House of Commons and in the House of Lords, and as he relied on Lord Ravenscar to inform him about the latter, long consultations resulted almost every morning at Carlton House.

When the Prince was not talking politics he was concerned with the behaviour of his wife.

Princess Caroline had now allied herself with her husband's political opponents, declaring that she was "proud to name herself a Pittite."

At Montague House she entertained Lord Elwin, the dismissed Lord Chancellor, Viscount Castlereagh, who had been Pitt's Secretary of State for War, and Spencer Perceval, who had resigned as Attorney General.

Lord Ravenscar had learnt that they had all dined with the Princess to decide what action should be taken against the Ministers who had undertaken on the Prince's behalf a "delicate investigation" into her conduct.

Lord Ravenscar had advised the Prince against doing anything in public which would result inevitably in people taking sides.

He knew how badly the Prince was treated by the cartoonists and the gossip-writers with regard to his marriage, and he could not help wondering if he might find himself in a similar position.

Supposing his own wife outraged the proprieties as Princess Caroline was doing? Supposing she thwarted him at every turn and went out of her way to make him look a fool in public?

Then he consoled himself with the thought it was most unlikely the General's daughter would be anything but discreet and well behaved.

At the same time, he saw in the Prince's affairs how he himself, having been carried away in his desire for revenge against Atalie, might have been in even a worse predicament than he was at the moment.

"I shall have to talk to Romara," he decided, "and get everything settled between us."

He thought that perhaps if he gave her enough money she might prefer to live apart from him. But that would be an uncomfortable state of affairs not only for himself but also for Romara.

There would be a time in the future when he would need a wife, and he had the idea that there were various appointments both in London and in the County to be offered him once it was thought that he had "settled down."

For almost the first time in his life Lord Ravenscar felt indecisive and not in complete control of his destiny.

He had always known exactly what he wanted and made sure that he had it. Atalie had been the first serious set-back he had ever encountered.

Even to think of her made him scowl and feel again a reflection of the anger she had caused when she jilted him.

He had learnt from some of her more intimate friends that she had been struck dumb when she had read of his marriage in *The Gazette*.

It was obvious, they had told Lord Ravenscar, that she had never envisaged such a thing could happen to her.

Quickly she had announced her own engagement, but that did not prevent a great deal of speculation as to what had happened taking place amongst their mutual friends.

Lord Ravenscar was of course questioned about

his wife by everybody who was brave enough to do so, and he found that a perfect excuse to explain her absence was to say that she was in deep mourning.

"I cannot help thinking," the Viscount said to him one evening when they were dining together, "that the General would be pleased if he knew that you were his son-in-law."

"He would certainly have had a very different feeling about Wychbold," Lord Ravenscar remarked dryly.

"Yes, I know, but you were always a favourite of his," the Viscount said reflectively.

"He certainly never showed it when I was in the Regiment," Lord Ravenscar replied. "I remember being 'dressed down' by him on various occasions, and a very unpleasant experience it was!"

"He was a martinet all right!" The Viscount laughed. "At the same time, the troops were ready to die for him—and I think we felt the same."

Later that evening as he got into bed Lord Ravenscar found himself saying beneath his breath:

"She is the General's daughter. Why then should I feel so apprehensive about the future?"

Nevertheless, he knew that he was afraid of two things: first, that Romara should prove to be as ugly as she had appeared on her wedding-day, and secondly that she should behave like Princess Caroline.

Although he would never have admitted it, Lord Ravenscar was unusually sensitive.

This was perhaps because he was an only child and had therefore been forced to use his imagination more than did children who had brothers and sisters with whom they could play.

It may also have been because he was so intelligent and well read.

Whatever the reason, he had deep feelings that he tried to hide even from himself, and as he journeyed towards his house in the country he became more introspective than another man might have been.

He had deliberately not told his Agent at what

time he would arrive, not wishing to tie himself down to leaving London at any particular time.

He suspected at the last moment that he might have to see Charles Grey, a close friend, who had become Viscount Howick in April and had been appointed First Lord of the Admiralty.

Charles, however, had sent a message to say that he would be engaged all the morning at a Cabinet Meeting, and Lord Ravenscar had therefore set off for Raven House earlier than he had expected.

He was driving a new team of horses that he had bought at Tattersall's the previous week. They were all perfectly matched, jet black with the exception of a white star on their foreheads.

They were so unusual and distinctive that every man turned to stare at them while they drove through the streets, while the women looked and looked again at the man who was driving them.

Lord Ravenscar was quite unaware of the admiration he was arousing, but drove rather faster than usual, as if he was in a hurry to reach his destination.

He was in fact anxious to face what lay ahead and get it over with.

The problem had lingered for too long at the back of his mind like a sleeping serpent and now he could delay the confrontation no longer.

The country after the heat of London was cool and beautiful and Lord Ravenscar wondered to himself why he did not spend more time at his ancestral home.

"I will arrange some shooting-parties in the autumn," he decided, and wondered if his wife would expect to play hostess to his friends.

The idea made his hackles rise and he thought he must make no decision of any sort until he had seen Romara and straightened out the position between them.

He reached Raven House about noon and thought it was looking even more beautiful than usual.

The garden was a riot of colour and he remembered how his mother had loved her rose-garden. He had not really appreciated the many improvements she had made in the garden and house until she was no longer there.

Raven House had in fact seemed horribly empty after her death, and because Lord Ravenscar missed her at times intolerably, it had resulted in his living almost exclusively in his house in Curzon Street.

As he walked into the Hall he knew he was tense, and as the Major Domo hurried forward, full of apologies at not being on the door-step, he said:

"I am earlier than I expected. Where is Her Ladyship?"

"I think Her Ladyship is in the Blue Salon, M'Lord. Shall I find out?"

"No," Lord Ravenscar answered. "I will look for myself."

He spoke sharply, and walked across the Hall to open the door of the Blue Salon, which had been his mother's favourite room and which looked out over the rose-garden.

At first glance he thought the room was empty, then he saw a woman dressed in white standing by the window.

She had her back to him and as he walked towards her he saw that she held a baby in her arms.

He thought it must be Caryl and remembered that she, thanks to his cleverness, was also "Her Ladyship."

As he reached the woman with the baby he was just about to greet her when she must have heard him and turned her head.

Lord Ravenscar found himself looking at the face of someone he had never seen before.

Oval in shape, with a pointed chin, it was dominated by two large eyes and between them a small, straight nose.

For one second he wondered who the lovely stranger could be, then as he saw the eyes light up and a smile part two attractively curved red lips, he realised it was his wife!

"My Lord!" Romara exclaimed. "We were not expecting you until the afternoon! Mr. Arkwright was sure you would be kept busy by your political friends."

"Nobody wanted me, so I got away early."

His reply was almost automatic, for he was finding it hard to do anything but stare at Romara.

Caryl was certainly pretty with her fair hair and blue eyes, but he realised that her sister had a distinction altogether her own.

There was something in her beauty to which for the moment Lord Ravenscar could not put a name.

As if she felt a little shy at his scrutiny, Romara looked down at the sleeping baby in her arms and said:

"May I introduce you to your latest guest? His name is to be Alexander, although I suspect we will call him Alex."

Lord Ravenscar forced himself to look at the baby she held against her breast.

"He is very small," he remarked, feeling that some comment was expected of him.

"He was in rather a hurry to arrive," Romara answered, "but he is growing. He is growing every day!"

There was a note of pride in her voice and she added:

"His mother dotes on him and is so much better in health than I ever expected she would be."

"So Arkwright has told me," Lord Ravenscar said. "In fact, in his letters he eulogises over this baby to such an extent that I rather suspect he is regretting the long years he has remained a bachelor."

Romara laughed.

"We shall have to find him a wife."

"I shall be extremely angry if you do!" Lord Ravenscar replied. "Arkwright is indispensable as my Agent, Manager, Secretary, factotum, and lastly, friend."

"And you think a wife would upset all that?" Romara enquired.

There was a silence, then Lord Ravenscar said in a different tone of voice:

"Even having seen Caryl, I did not expect you

to be so lovely—or perhaps 'beautiful' is the right word!"

He saw the colour rise in Romara's cheeks, and he liked the way her eyes were suddenly shy and unable to meet his.

He was used to women who accepted compliments as their right. He was used too to the bold, inviting glances of those who were only too anxious not only to captivate but also to capture him.

"The . . . bruises are . . . gone," Romara said in a low voice, "but I am . . . afraid there is still a . . . scar on my cheek."

"I can hardly see it," Lord Ravenscar said truthfully.

"That is entirely due to Mrs. Fellows," Romara told him. "Do you know, she told me there was a belief amongst the country-folk where she comes from that oil from wheat will remove scars."

She smiled and a small dimple appeared in one cheek as she went on:

"I am afraid we crushed and pounded quite a lot of Your Lordship's good grain to obtain enough oil, but it certainly seems to be very efficacious."

"Perhaps we should think of it as an honourable wound received in battle."

"It is not a battle I wish to remember," Romara replied.

The baby made a little sound and she said:

"I must take Alex back to his mother. We have been in the garden for a short while, but now Caryl has gone upstairs to lie down. The Doctor insists that she must have plenty of rest."

"Of course!" Lord Ravenscar agreed. "But I hope you will be able to have luncheon with me."

"I should like that," Romara answered.

She smiled at him and moved across the Salon with a grace that made him think of his mother.

Then as if he felt in need of air he walked out onto the terrace to look down at the rose-garden.

How could he have imagined it? How could he have dreamt that he would be so fortunate?

Having married what he believed to be the ugliest woman in London, he was unbelievably lucky to have found first that she was not a prostitute, as she might so easily have been, but his own General's daughter.

Secondly, and perhaps more important, he now found that she was beautiful with a loveliness that was unusual and perhaps unique.

He confirmed this opinion in his mind as they talked together during luncheon, discussing mainly politics, in which he found that Romara was surprisingly knowledgeable.

She told him that her father had always been politically minded and when he was ill she had read aloud to him all the Parliamentary Reports in the newspapers.

Then he had liked to discuss various aspects of them, expecting her to have an opinion, even if it differed from his own.

Lord Ravenscar therefore found himself relating not only what had happened in Parliament, which Romara could read for herself, but what had occurred at many of the Conferences in which he had taken part.

He also told her some things which had been related to him privately by his friends, like the Earl Spencer, who had become Home Secretary.

Romara listened to every word he had to say with undisguised interest, and her intelligent questions made him find with surprise that they had lingered over luncheon for quite a considerable time.

As she rose to her feet she said apologetically:

"I am afraid I have kept you from the things you must want to do. I am sorry, but it is so fascinating talking to somebody who knows as much as you do and can tell me all the things I have always longed to hear."

It flashed through Lord Ravenscar's mind that Atalie had never shown the slightest interest in politics, or, if it came to that, in anything but herself.

"What do you intend to do this afternoon?" he asked.

"I was thinking of visiting Westons' Farm," Romara answered.

Lord Ravenscar looked surprised, and she explained quickly:

"Mr. Arkwright told me that Mrs. Weston is ill, so I was going to take her some soup, and some flowers which I picked this morning."

She paused, looking embarrassed, and added:

"I think really that she had told Mr. Arkwright how much she wants to meet me."

Lord Ravenscar laughed.

"I am quite certain that all the tenants are agog with curiosity about you."

"I have not been able to visit anyone until my face was better," Romara said, "but I hope to meet them all . . . that is, if you . . . approve."

She looked at him anxiously, as if she expected him to say that he had no wish for her to ingratiate herself with his tenants, but Lord Ravenscar answered quietly:

"I feel sure I can rely on you to do the right thing."

He thought that Romara's eyes lit up, and she said:

"The farmer's wife whom I called on yesterday said some very delightful things about your mother. She must have been a wonderful person. I have learnt that they all loved her on the estate."

"And she loved them," Lord Ravenscar replied.

As Romara left the Dining-Room and went towards the Salon, he thought that she was unlike any other woman he had brought to Raven House or, for that matter, any woman he had known in London. She seemed to "fit in."

He had a strange thought that the house had accepted her. Aloud he said:

"Why not forget the soup? Somebody else can take that, and we might ride over together to the farm. I wanted to see Weston to find out what crops he is planting for next year. George Spencer is certain that the country will have to grow more food if we are to be at war for any length of time."

"Surely it will not last long?" Romara asked.

Then she gave a little sigh before she went on:

"I suppose really there is no-one strong enough to defeat Napoleon."

"We will defeat him in the end," Lord Ravenscar said positively, "but it will not be easy and victory will not come quickly."

"I hate to think of men being killed and of all the suffering there is on the Continent."

"War always means suffering."

Romara did not answer, and as if she tried to sweep away the momentary unhappiness his words had caused her, she asked:

"If we are going riding, shall I go and change?"

"I will order the horses to be round in half-an-hour," he replied.

"I will not take as long as that!" Romara answered. "But I must first tell Caryl where we are going."

She ran up the stairs in a way which told Lord Ravenscar that she was excited at what lay ahead.

When half-an-hour later they set off across the Park to Westons' Farm, which was situated some two miles away, he knew by the light in her eyes and the smile on her lips that she was enjoying herself.

"You ride superbly!" he said after they had galloped for a short while, then drew in their horses to a slower pace.

"You could not have paid me a nicer compliment."

"I suppose it is what I might have expected of you, being your father's daughter. The General was always a good judge of horse-flesh."

"He was very particular about the horses he rode," Romara said, "and I had well-bred horses to ride even when I was a child."

She gave Lord Ravenscar a little smile as she added:

"They were good, but not as good as yours. I am thrilled with everything I have found in your stables."

"I will take you one day to see my race-horses,"

Lord Ravenscar promised. "I have some in training now at Newmarket and some at Epsom."

"I would love that!" Romara replied. "How many important races have you won?"

Horses kept them talking all the way to the farm.

Lord Ravenscar did not miss the easy, friendly manner in which Romara talked to the farmer and his wife and the way in which she seemed to be perfectly at home with them, just as his mother had been.

When they turned to go, Mrs. Weston, who was confined to a couch and unable to get to her feet, held on to Lord Ravenscar's hand.

"Oi wants t' wish Ye' Lordship every 'appiness," she said. "Though Oi know'd ye'd be fortunate the minute Oi set eyes on th' pretty lady ye've made yer wife. Jus' like yer mother, she be. There be no mistakin' the likeness, th' way she talks and th' things she says. It warms me 'eart to see ye both together!"

Lord Ravenscar, who had known Mrs. Weston ever since he was a small boy, thanked her.

Yet, riding home, he could not help wondering if Atalie or any other women of his acquaintance could have captivated the old country-folk in just such a charming manner.

Back at the house, Mr. Arkwright appeared with innumerable problems regarding the estate, and Romara slipped away, leaving them alone.

Lord Ravenscar did not see her again until dinner-time, and while he was dressing he remembered that the reason he had come to the country was to discuss with Romara their future.

Now he found himself wondering what there was to discuss.

She had settled down at Raven House in a manner he had not expected. There seemed no hurry to make plans, but better to leave things just as they were.

As his Valet helped him dress he found himself looking forward to the evening and remembering one or two interesting political anecdotes that he thought would amuse Romara and make her laugh.

She was waiting for him in the Salon when he came downstairs and he saw that she was wearing a very attractive gown which had undoubtedly been extremely expensive.

She must have sensed what he was thinking because with a little flush on her cheeks she said:

"You may think it . . . strange that I am not wearing mourning for Papa, but I thought it might depress Caryl, and I am therefore wearing one of her gowns, as I did not like to send home for my own."

"I think that was very sensible," Lord Ravenscar said, "but of course you must buy anything you require for yourself. That is one of the things I meant to talk about with you this evening."

"I have . . . money of my own," Romara said quickly. "Papa left me everything he possessed. It was not very much . . . as he always said, 'Soldiers cannot save money'."

She paused, then went on:

"However, he left nothing for Caryl because he was so angry with her for running away with Sir Harvey."

As she spoke Romara looked a little anxiously at Lord Ravenscar, in case what she had to say would annoy him. Then she said with what he knew was an effort:

"I want . . . if you agree . . . to give Caryl half of . . . everything Papa left me."

There was no doubt that she was afraid of what his reaction might be.

She knew that legally he had control of everything she possessed, and, as they were married, he should already have made an effort to consult the General's Solicitors.

"Let me make this quite clear, Romara," he replied. "Whatever money your father has left you is your own, and as far as I am concerned you may do with it as you wish. I shall give you, as my wife, a suitable allowance for your clothes and any further expenses you may incur."

"No . . . please . . . you must not . . . do that," Romara said quickly.

"Why not?" Lord Ravenscar enquired.

"You have been so kind . . . so very understanding . . . I cannot take any . . . more from you."

"That is a ridiculous argument!" he retorted. "Of course you must have money, and that is one of the things we have to settle together."

Romara looked at him as if she was trying to find a reason for his generosity. Then she said in a very low voice:

"I thought perhaps when Caryl is . . . well enough, you would like us to . . . go . . . back to Huntingdonshire."

"I have no wish for you to do anything of the sort!" Lord Ravenscar said positively, and he was surprised to hear the decisive note in his voice.

They dined alone because, as Romara explained, Caryl, on the Doctor's instructions, had not yet been down to dinner.

"I did hope that Caryl would want to see you," she said, "and make an effort, but I think actually she feels shy."

"Shy?" Lord Ravenscar questioned.

"She is so ashamed of having caused so much trouble and having the baby as soon as she arrived."

"It did not trouble me," Lord Ravenscar replied.

Romara gave a little laugh at the way he spoke. Then she said:

"Caryl felt embarrassed at upsetting your household the moment she stepped into it. As a matter of fact, they are all infatuated with Alexander, and if he stays here for long I am afraid he will be terribly spoilt."

"He may stay as long as you wish to have him here," Lord Ravenscar said, "and that applies also to his mother."

"You are so very . . . kind . . . I do not know . . . quite what to say," Romara murmured.

"Why not leave everything to me?" Lord Ravenscar suggested. "I am sure your father always made the decisions in your house. Well, I would like to make them in mine."

"Are you . . . quite certain you wish . . . us to stay?"

Lord Ravenscar did not miss the little pause before the word "us" and knew she had been about to say "me."

"When the Season is over and the Prince goes to Brighton, which he intends to do, I shall come home," Lord Ravenscar said. "Then we will have plenty of time, Romara, to talk about ourselves. As it is, I have discovered that you are both well and happy, and you must forgive me if I return to London tomorrow morning."

"Yes, of course," she said quickly.

They talked of many things over dinner and Romara told him how her mother had found it lonely when she had to remain in Huntingdonshire with her children while the General was away at the wars.

"He did not like us with him even when the Regiment was in England," Romara said, "and yet he loved my mother, and she adored him."

"I suppose," Lord Ravenscar said thoughtfully, "that was the sort of marriage you envisaged for yourself."

"To a soldier?" she asked.

"To a man who loved you," he answered.

She looked away from him, across the room. With his eyes on her profile, he thought how attractive was her small, straight nose, and how fortunate it was that it had not been broken by Sir Harvey's fist.

"I suppose to . . . marry someone one loves . . . deeply is what every woman . . . imagines will happen and longs for," Romara said at length.

"And that is something out of which you have been cheated," Lord Ravenscar said.

As if she refused to dwell on her own suffering, she answered:

"The same applies to you. It may have been your own . . . fault, but even if you could not marry the girl you really . . . loved, you certainly did not wish to be saddled with a stranger."

"I have been thinking today of how fortunate, in

fact, I have been," Lord Ravenscar said. "The stranger might have been very different from you, and the foolish way in which I lost my temper might have ruined my whole life."

Romara appeared to consider what he had said.

The servants when they left the room had extinguished the candles on the serving-table, so the only light came from those in the silver candelabra on the table.

Romara and Lord Ravenscar were, as it were, alone in a small island, surrounded by a darkness which shut them off from everything else.

Romara looked very lovely, and finally after there had been some seconds of silence she raised her eyes.

"It is kind of you to say that," she said. "At the same time, I am . . . ready to do . . . anything you wish . . . to go away . . . to stay . . . to try, if it is possible, to set you free."

"There is no way you can do that," Lord Ravenscar replied. "We were married legally, and I believe Joshua Meeding has registered the marriage."

"I have been . . . wondering if there was . . . any way out for you. I have a . . . feeling there must be . . . something that you could do."

"Are you thinking of me or of yourself?" Lord Ravenscar enquired.

"I was . . . really thinking . . . of you," Romara replied, and he knew she spoke the truth. "You have so much to give your . . . wife . . . I do not mean only possessions or wealth . . . I mean your brain . . ."

She hesitated and then finished:

"And all the . . . things that make up . . . you!"

"I think you are flattering me."

"No, I am being serious," Romara insisted. "Just as I wanted to marry someone I . . . loved, I think, because you are . . . different from many . . . men, you would not be . . . content with an . . . arranged marriage; a marriage that just brought you land or wealth."

She paused before she said rather shyly:

"I have a feeling . . . you must not think it impertinent of me... that the reason you have not married before is because you have never been... in love... in an idealistic way."

Lord Ravenscar remembered what he had felt about Atalie and how she was in fact the first woman he had ever really considered as his wife.

"That is true," he said, "but I now realise such ideas are childish and belong only to the Romantics."

"No, you must not feel like that!" Romara cried. "If you become bitter and cynical because of what has happened, that will change you."

"Would that matter?" Lord Ravenscar enquired.

"Yes, it would!" she said passionately. "How can you let someone who is not really worthy of you ruin your life?"

"Not—worthy of me?" Lord Ravenscar asked quietly. "What do you know about the woman I wished to marry?"

The colour rose in Romara's face.

"Tell me!" he insisted. "I wish to know!"

"You may think it very... ill-bred of me," Romara said in a small voice. "But Mrs. Fellows, who has known you ever since you were a small boy, has talked to me and told me so... many things about ... you."

"And apparently about Atalie Bray," Lord Ravenscar added.

He did not know why, but he wished to force from Romara what information she had received about the woman who had been instrumental in causing their marriage.

"Perhaps I should not have been... curious about her," Romara said a little uncomfortably, "but I was."

"I am still waiting for you to tell me what you know."

"Mrs. Fellows said she was... beautiful, the most beautiful person she had ever seen."

"Is that all?"

"You may not... like what else she said."

"Like it or not, I still wish to hear it," Lord Ravenscar insisted.

"S-she said that servants talk and she had heard

things about Miss Bray that made her f-feel she would not make you the . . . sort of wife you . . . should have."

Lord Ravenscar did not speak and Romara said quickly:

"You must not be annoyed with Mrs. Fellows. I should not have . . . told you what she said, but she loves you. She loves you with a whole-hearted devotion and she thinks you are the most wonderful man that ever stepped on this earth!"

Lord Ravenscar was astonished.

"I feel you must be exaggerating."

Romara shook her head.

"All the servants here love you because they have watched you grow up, and they feel that in a way you . . . belong to them just as they belong to . . . you. That is what makes this house such a happy one."

Lord Ravenscar sighed.

"It was when my mother was alive, but now . . ."

"I think it is only waiting for you to come back and live here," Romara said, "and that it should be cared for by the . . . right person."

"Mrs. Fellows and the other staff seem to think that Atalie Bray was not 'the right person'?"

"It is better for me not to answer that question."

"I insist on your answering it," Lord Ravenscar said firmly. "You have said so much, you cannot back out now. Tell me the truth, Romara, and perhaps it will help me to have more common sense than I have shown in the past."

He was obviously determined upon having an answer, and finally Romara said in a low voice:

"Mrs. Fellows and the rest of your staff who met . . . her thought Miss Bray was selfish and also rude to the servants when she was . . . alone with them. In fact . . . if you want the truth . . . they hated her!"

Lord Ravenscar looked astonished.

He realised it had never struck him that servants, who were just there when one wanted them, should have such strong feelings about anyone, especially himself.

Then he thought that the reason why he was so comfortable, well looked after, and surrounded by those he could trust was that his household was staffed by those his mother had chosen and who carried on the same traditions as when she was alive.

It suddenly struck him that as the old servants died off it would be hard to replace them with those of the same quality and calibre.

"I am . . . sorry if what I said seemed . . . impertinent," Romara was saying, "but you did make me tell you."

"You have been frank with me, Romara," Lord Ravenscar answered, "and that is something I hope you will always be. If there is one thing I really dislike it is being lied to or deceived."

"I can understand that," Romara said, "and I will never lie. But there is no reason always to volunteer the truth. As my Nanny used to say: 'What one doesn't know, one cannot grieve over.' "

Lord Ravenscar laughed. Then as if he thought of it for the first time, he said:

"Has Arkwright found a Nurse for your sister's baby?"

"There was no need to look far." Romara smiled. "Mrs. Fellows's younger sister, who has always been in the Nursery of one grand house or another, was only too eager to come back here."

"To come back?" Lord Ravenscar queried.

"She was a Nursery-maid when you were in the cradle."

They both laughed; then, leaving the Dining-Room, they walked together into the Salon.

"You do not wish port?" Romara asked.

"I am cutting down on my drinking," Lord Ravenscar replied. "It has got me into enough trouble as it is."

"I am sure that is wise," she said.

As she spoke she looked at him in a mischievous way, as if she was amused at the care he was taking of himself.

It was dark outside and although the servants had lit the candles they had not drawn the curtains over the long French window which opened onto the terrace.

Romara walked outside to look at the pink glow behind the high trees in the Park, which was the last of the setting sun. It made the fountain that was playing in the centre of the rose-garden shimmer with colour.

"It is all so lovely," she said. "More beautiful than I thought any house could be."

"I am glad it pleases you," Lord Ravenscar replied, "as it will be your home in the future."

He knew as he spoke that it was not an idle phrase. He had made up his mind that Romara was his wife. There would be no further talk of evading the marriage or of living separate lives.

As if she understood what he was saying, she looked at him gravely.

"What I want you to do," he said, "is exactly what you are doing already. Get to know my people, the farmers, the tenants, everyone connected with the estate, and when your sister is stronger, then you and I can make plans for her future. But let me make it quite clear that she will always be welcome in my house."

Romara made a little gesture with her hand as if she would touch him, then she said:

"Sometimes . . . in the night I wake up in a sudden terror . . . thinking that after what . . . Sir Harvey did to me I am not . . . married to you but to some . . . monster of a m-man like him . . . or worse."

"You are quite certain that has not happened?" Lord Ravenscar asked.

His question swept away the seriousness from Romara's face.

"Of course," she said in a different tone, "there is still time to discover that you are really a Bluebeard in disguise and have a dozen decapitated wives hidden away in the cellar, or, with their heads still on, imprisoned in the attic!"

"The search will undoubtedly occupy you until I return," Lord Ravenscar replied.

"You are making it very . . . difficult for me to say the things I meant to say," Romara murmured.

"What are they?" he enquired.

"Mostly a profusion of thanks and a willingness to . . . disappear out of your life . . . if that was what you would . . . prefer."

"Now you know I prefer nothing of the sort!" Lord Ravenscar said sharply. "And even if I did, it would be impossible for either of us to lead such a life forever. We have to be practical, Romara, and both of us have to make the best of a bad job—if that is what it is."

"As I have said already, I will do . . . anything you . . . tell me to . . . do."

"I wonder if such submissiveness will last," Lord Ravenscar said provocatively.

She knew that he was teasing her and there was a mischievous twinkle in her own eyes as she said:

"Only time can answer that question for you."

"That is true," he said with a smile.

"I will say good-night," Romara told him, "because I know that Mr. Arkwright has left a great many letters for you to approve in the Library. But I shall hope that I may see you at breakfast before you leave for London."

"I shall be very disappointed if you do not bid me good-bye," Lord Ravenscar replied.

"Then good-night, My Lord."

Romara curtseyed and he took her hand in his and raised it to his lips.

He did not kiss it perfunctorily as was customary but instead his lips touched the softness of her skin and lingered there for a moment.

He felt that she drew in her breath in surprise, then she moved swiftly away through the open window and he was alone.

He stood looking out over the rose-garden, remembering that when he had thought of Atalie as his wife he had always meant to bring her here.

He had thought that she would look her most beautiful against the background of the house, the roses, the mystery of the trees, and the silver of the lake.

Just for a moment some part of him cried out for his lost dream.

Then he found himself thinking of how soft Romara's skin had been when his lips touched it.

Chapter Five

Lord Ravenscar came to breakfast early but there was no sign of Romara, and in fact he had almost finished when she came into the room.

"Good-morning, Romara," he said, rising to his feet.

He intended to tease her about being late, then he saw her face.

"What has happened?" he asked.

She came slowly to the table and sat down, waving away the food the servants offered to her.

Then as they withdrew she said:

"A letter came for Caryl this morning."

"A letter?" Lord Ravenscar repeated.

"Fortunately I was with her when it was brought to her, and as she was feeding the baby she took no notice of it."

Romara handed the letter to Lord Ravenscar, which she had concealed in her lap, and went on:

"As it looked official, I opened it. You will see what it says."

He knew by the expression on her face and the tone of her voice that something momentous had occurred.

He took the letter from her and saw at once that it was from a firm of Solicitors and addressed to Caryl.

Briefly, on behalf of Sir Harvey they called upon

her to return immediately to her husband's house, bringing their son with her.

Lord Ravenscar thought he might have anticipated that Sir Harvey would react in such a manner. Then he read on:

If Your Ladyship does not comply with this request within a reasonable period of time, Sir Harvey will appeal to the Courts for the possession and custody of his son and will take steps to prove that the child's mother is not a fit and proper person to have the care of him.

As Romara saw that Lord Ravenscar's eyes had reached the bottom of the page, she asked in a voice little above a whisper:

"Can he do . . . that?"

"I must be truthful and say that there is nothing to stop him," Lord Ravenscar replied.

"You mean . . . he would go into Court and say that because Caryl was living with him for so long before they were . . . married, she is an . . . immoral woman?"

Romara could hardly breathe the words, and yet they were said.

"That is what he is threatening," Lord Ravenscar answered quietly.

He was surprised that Romara should have such a quick grasp of the situation. At the same time, he knew it was very serious.

A wife belonged to her husband and he was also the father of his children.

Sir Harvey therefore was completely justified in asking for his wife to return to him, and a refusal could result in his evoking the law in the way in which he had threatened.

Moreover, Lord Ravenscar had the uncomfortable feeling that if Sir Harvey did so he would win.

The law was biased entirely in favour of the man, and for a woman to be branded as immoral would damn her completely from the very opening of the case.

As if she knew what thoughts were passing through his mind Romara asked:

"What can we do... about it? Oh, please... help! I am sure you can think of some... solution."

Lord Ravenscar wished that he was as confident as she was of his ability to find a way out of what seemed to him a complete impasse.

Then, because Romara sounded so distressed, he said soothingly:

"I promise you that as soon as I arrive in London I will consult my own Solicitors about this threat. They are considered to be the very best in Lincoln's Inn."

"Oh, thank you," Romara said. "I am so sorry to trouble you... further, but I know that if... anyone can... help, it will be... you!"

She was leaning towards him as she spoke.

Looking at her troubled eyes, with a suspicion of tears in them, at her pale face and her lips, which trembled, Lord Ravenscar had an almost uncontrollable impulse to put his arms round her, to kiss her and tell her not to worry.

His desire to do so was so violent that it was only with difficulty that he took his eyes from her to say abruptly:

"Leave everything to me and try not to worry. You were right not to tell Caryl about this letter."

"I think it would... kill her if she had to... lose Alexander," Romara murmured.

"I will do everything in my power to see that that does not happen!" Lord Ravenscar swore.

As he spoke, Mr. Arkwright came into the Dining-Room, and because he had no wish for his Agent to know that anything was amiss, he asked in a different tone of voice:

"What have you planned to do today?"

"I expect we will just sit in the garden," Romara replied, "but I shall miss riding with you."

"I shall miss it too," Lord Ravenscar replied.

Then he held out his hand for the papers which Mr. Arkwright had brought to him.

"If you would be kind enough, My Lord, to

have these delivered to the Solicitors," Mr. Arkwright said, "they will be properly stamped and registered."

"I shall take them myself," Lord Ravenscar said. "I wish to call there anyway."

He knew that Romara would be glad that he had a reason for going to Lincoln's Inn anyway, and therefore would not be so conscious that she was once again imposing on his kindness.

Mr. Arkwright left the room, and Lord Ravenscar, rising to his feet, said:

"The sooner I get to London the better! Look after yourself. I do not like to think of you being unhappy."

"I feel so much better now that I have told you about it," Romara said simply.

They walked side by side into the Hall. Outside the front door, Lord Ravenscar's Phaeton with his new jet-black team was waiting for him.

At the bottom of the steps he took her hand and lifted it to his lips, but he did not kiss it in the same manner as he had done last night. Instead, she felt a firm pressure of his fingers, as if to reassure her.

Then he climbed into the driver's seat, and as he raised his hat the horses were moving across the gravel in front of the house.

Romara watched until Lord Ravenscar was out of sight; then, with a little sigh, she went upstairs to find Caryl.

It seemed impossible that so many problems and difficulties could have arisen since she had travelled to London at her sister's request, and she wondered what would have happened if Lord Ravenscar had not been there to help them.

For one thing, Alexander would have been born without a name.

For another, she could not help feeling at the back of her mind that because Sir Harvey had not allowed Caryl to make any preparations for the baby's birth, it might in fact have killed her.

It was a terrible thing to think about anyone doing, and yet Romara was certain that Sir Harvey would stop at nothing to get his own way.

That was why now she was so afraid, and she could understand that he would use every means in his power to gain possession of his son and heir.

'Oh, God, please let Lord Ravenscar help us,' Romara prayed in her heart.

Then, forcing a smile to her lips, she went into the Nursery, where Caryl was with Alexander.

* * *

It was a week before Lord Ravenscar returned, arriving at home so late that Romara had already gone to bed.

He had hoped to get away early but had been unavoidably detained, so that it was already late in the evening before he was able to leave London.

There was however plenty of light for him to see his way, because they had not yet reached the longest day of the year and the roads were comparatively empty of traffic.

At the same time, he regretted that he would not be able to talk to Romara that evening as he had wished to do. He had a great deal to tell her, but unfortunately none of it was good news.

His Solicitors, very experienced and spoken of as the best in London, had been in contact with Sir Harvey's Advisers only to find, as they had told Lord Ravenscar, that they were "up against a brick wall."

"I gather the gentleman in question, My Lord, is very obstinate and not prepared to negotiate as we had hoped."

It was what Lord Ravenscar had expected, but it was a blow to hear it put so bluntly.

He realised now that in closing to Sir Harvey all the doors to the Social World, he had left himself without an inducement with which he could bribe him.

Sir Harvey was rich, so it was not a question of money, and, had he not been humiliated in the way he had by the Viscount and his friends after the wedding-ceremony, there was just a chance that he might have been more amenable.

Lord Ravenscar could not help thinking that Sir Harvey was not only forcing Caryl to obey him but being deliberately unpleasant to her sister and himself.

He would be well aware who had actually arranged his marriage with Caryl and he would guess that there had been communications between his household and that of his next-door neighbour.

Lord Ravenscar had told his Solicitors to make further representation, and then decided that Romara must know what had happened so far.

He was well aware of how anxious she would be, and somehow he could not get out of his mind the expression of trust in her troubled eyes when she had looked at him at the breakfast-table.

"I have to find a way to help her," he told himself, and pushed his horses in an effort to reach Raven House as quickly as possible.

Even so, the house was in darkness when he arrived and he learnt that Romara had gone to bed.

As he undressed in the room next to hers it struck him that he had only to open the communicating-door to be beside her.

After all, he was her husband, and she was his wife, and there would be nothing wrong in approaching her.

Then he told himself that she might be shocked or apprehensive, and that would spoil the friendly relationship they had with each other so far.

'It is too soon to take any chances,' he thought.

Then he was surprised to realise how much he actually wanted to see her.

He told himself that it was only because he disliked the thought of her being worried and unhappy, and yet he knew, if he was truthful, that it was more than that and somehow her problems had become very much a part of him.

He got up early the next morning, and this time

when he came down to breakfast Romara was there before him.

She rose from the table as he came into the Dining-Room and said with a little lilt in her voice:

"I heard you were back, My Lord. I wish I had known you were coming. I would have waited up for you."

"I was not sure until the last moment that I could get away," Lord Ravenscar said, "and, as it was so late, I did not like to disturb you."

"I would not have minded," Romara said.

They both sat down and she said in a low voice:

"It has been a very long week . . . waiting to hear from you."

There was a little throb in her voice that he did not miss. Then, as the servants offered him a dish, he said to relieve the obvious tension:

"Arkwright told me that you and Caryl were in good health and that Alexander was growing into a giant, so I assumed all was well."

"Caryl is very happy," Romara said.

"I hope I shall be able to see her on this visit."

"She is looking forward to it, and of course she wants to thank you for all you have done for her."

"You must tell her that gratitude bores me," Lord Ravenscar replied, "but I shall look forward to meeting you both at dinner."

Romara looked surprised, and he explained:

"Did Arkwright not tell you that he particularly wanted me back as soon as possible to discuss the digging of a gravel-pit on the northern border of the estate?"

"I think he must have mentioned it," Romara said, "but to be honest, I was not very interested in gravel."

"Nor am I," Lord Ravenscar replied, "but apparently it is urgently needed in the County, and I have to see the men concerned."

Romara thought wistfully that she would have liked to ride to the northern border of the estate with him, but she was quite certain that this was an all-male meeting and she would be very out of place at it.

Because she did not wish Lord Ravenscar to know how disappointed she was that he would spend the day away from home, she said lightly:

"Actually, Caryl and I had planned a picnic today down by the lake. It is so beautiful there and we thought one of the servants could carry our luncheon down for us and bring it back later."

"That is a very good idea," Lord Ravenscar said. "It is what I remember doing when I was a child."

"So Mrs. Fellows told me."

"So it is traditional once again." He smiled. "We cannot get away from it, can we?"

"I have no wish to do so," Romara said softly.

The Butler stopped beside Lord Ravenscar's chair.

"Can Mr. Arkwright speak to you for a moment, M'Lord?"

"But of course!" Lord Ravenscar replied. "Tell him to come in."

Mr. Arkwright entered the room.

"Good-morning, My Lady. Good-morning, My Lord."

Romara smiled at him.

"I have just learnt," he said, speaking to her, "that you are planning to picnic down by the lake today."

"Yes, I was just telling His Lordship about it."

"I would much rather you did not go so far from the house."

"Why ever not?" Romara enquired in surprise.

"I learnt yesterday from one of the farmers that a large dog has been chasing the sheep and also the deer in the Park. They think it has gone mad with the heat, and although they have tried to shoot him they have so far been unsuccessful."

"You need not worry about us," Romara said. "Just give me a gun."

"Give you a gun?" Mr. Arkwright repeated. "Can Your Ladyship shoot?"

"As it happens, I am a very good shot," Romara

replied, "although perhaps it is conceited of me to say so! But because we lived in an isolated part of Huntingdonshire and my father was so often away from home, he insisted that we should all be able to handle a shot-gun and a pistol."

She turned to smile at Lord Ravenscar as she added:

"One day when you have time I will challenge Your Lordship to a shooting-match with a target as many yards away as you choose."

"I shall certainly take you up on that," Lord Ravenscar laughed, "and the prize must make it worthwhile."

"That will be even more exciting!" Romara exclaimed.

Her eyes met Lord Ravenscar's and it seemed for a moment as if they were saying things to each other that Mr. Arkwright could not understand.

Then, almost with an effort, Romara turned to the Agent to say:

"I think both you and His Lordship can trust me to look after Caryl and Alexander. I have no wish to forgo the picnic."

Mr. Arkwright looked to Lord Ravenscar for instruction.

"Give Her Ladyship one of my smaller duelling-pistols, Arkwright."

"Yes, of course, My Lord."

Mr. Arkwright went from the room and Lord Ravenscar said:

"I was thinking a little while ago that it would be fun to have some shooting-parties here in the autumn. Will you play hostess to them?"

"You know that I would be very proud to do so," Romara answered.

"We will think of some amusing guests."

He rose and as she did so he added:

"I suppose Arkwright will be waiting for me, but you ought to stay and have some breakfast."

"I hoped we would have a chance to talk."

"We will do that as soon as I return," Lord Ravenscar promised. "I have a lot to tell you, but I am afraid it is not exactly what you want to hear."

"Bad news?"

"Shall we say not good—not so far, anyway."

She gave a deep sigh.

"I was afraid that was what you would say."

"There is no reason to give up hope," Lord Ravenscar said. "I knew you would be worrying, otherwise I would not have returned until I had something more encouraging to tell you."

"I am so glad that you are here," she said simply.

Once again their eyes met, and Romara felt that she was telling him how desperately she had prayed every night that he would find a way of saving Caryl.

Sometimes her prayers grew muddled and she was not quite certain if she was praying to him or to God.

"I will get back as early as I can, Romara," Lord Ravenscar said. "I expect Caryl rests in the afternoon; then you and I can be alone and I will tell you everything I know."

"I shall look forward to that."

"And so shall I."

She walked with him towards the Hall and when they reached it Mr. Arkwright came hurrying towards them from the direction of the Gun-Room.

"Here is a pistol, Your Ladyship," he said. "But please be careful, because it is loaded."

"I promise you I know how to handle firearms," Romara said reassuringly. "My father was furious if any of us was not what he called 'safe.'"

"If you should see the dog, please shoot it," Mr. Arkwright said. "It has already done a great deal of damage, and the farmers with sheep will be very grateful to you."

"It is not something I shall enjoy doing," Romara replied, "but I understand the necessity for it."

"I think actually you will be putting it out of its misery," Mr. Arkwright said.

Then he hurried after Lord Ravenscar, who was already mounted on the horse that had been waiting for him outside the front door.

Romara waved as they rode away, and Lord

Ravenscar, looking back, thought that she looked very graceful in her white gown silhouetted against the grey stone of the house.

Once again he thought how well she fitted in and how she already seemed to be a part of his household as if she had always been there.

Then he told himself that this evening he would have a long talk with her not only about the things that concerned Caryl but also those that concerned themselves.

* * *

It was a very hot day, but under the green trees down beside the lake it was cool, and the dragonflies, iridescent over the silver water, gave it a fairy-like enchantment.

Footmen had carried down the picnic-basket and laid out a cold luncheon that looked delicious on a white linen cloth.

They had brought cushions on which Romara and Caryl could sit and prop their backs against the trees.

Caryl laid the baby down on a cushion, pulled the shawl away from his arms, and pulled up his long lace-edged dress so that he could kick his legs.

"Very soon he will be crawling," she said.

"Oh, do not let him grow up too quickly!" Romara pleaded. "He is so sweet as he is."

"He is beautiful!" Caryl said in a rapturous voice. "And I love him!"

She gave a little laugh as if at the intensity of her feelings and added lightly:

"I will make him a daisy-chain. Do you remember how we used to make them as children and thought how when we put them on our heads we looked like the Queen of the Fairies?"

"We have all the fairy-stories at home that Mama used to read to us," Romara said. "I am sure Alexander will love them when he is older."

It seemed as if Alexander was enjoying the picnic. When he was awake he gurgled happily at the sun-kissed leaves of the trees over his head.

Caryl and Romara talked for a little while of when they were children, then Romara said:

"I am going to walk to the edge of the lake and see if there are any fish."

"I will come with you," Caryl said.

She looked at Alexander and saw that he had fallen asleep.

"He will be all right," she said.

Taking Romara by the hand, they walked along the edge of the lake until they found a spot where they could peer through the thick rushes and see into the clear water.

"There are fish!" Romara said excitedly. "They look like trout. We must ask Mr. Arkwright about them. It would be great fun to catch some. I wonder if His Lordship ever fishes for them."

There were so many things, she thought, which she wanted to know about the man she had married and who owned what she was quite certain was the most beautiful house in England.

She knew that Mrs. Fellows was only too willing to talk interminably about "Master Trent," as she often called him absentmindedly, but it was more thrilling to talk to Lord Ravenscar himself and hear not only what he had done in his life but what he thought.

"He is very clever," Romara had told herself. "I do hope he does not find me a bore."

At the back of her mind there was always the picture of Atalie Bray, "the most beautiful girl in England," the woman to whom Lord Ravenscar had given his heart.

However she had behaved, however much she had angered him, Romara was sure that he still loved her.

After all, love did not die so easily, and she told herself that it would take a very, very, long time for him to forget Atalie, if he ever did so.

The thought was depressing, and she turned to say something to Caryl and as she did so she looked to where they had been sitting, and saw, to her astonishment, a strange man picking up Alexander.

Caryl saw what was happening at the same time and gave a little cry.

"What are you doing? You must not touch him!" she shouted, and moved forward.

The man looked towards them and Romara thought he had a dark, sinister-looking face.

Then, clutching the baby closely to him, he turned and started to run away through the trees.

Even as he did so Romara knew what was happening. This was Sir Harvey's man and he was taking Alexander away.

"Stop! Stop!" Caryl was crying frantically. "You are stealing my baby!"

Romara did not waste her breath in crying out. She merely ran quicker than she had ever run before in her whole life.

Lying on the grass beside the picnic-hamper was the pistol, where she had laid it.

She picked it up; then, running between the nearest trees, she had a view of the man who was carrying Alexander hurrying away.

He was already quite some distance from her, but Romara without even stopping to think brought down her pistol in the way her father had taught her and pulled the trigger!

There was a resounding report and she thought for a moment that she had missed. Then the man, still running, stumbled, swayed for a moment, and fell.

Before Romara could reach him Caryl was there first, snatching up Alexander, who was screaming lustily on the grass.

Fortunately, he had been thrown forwards and was not smothered beneath the falling man as he might have been.

With her baby clasped in her arms, Caryl, white-faced, turned to look at her sister.

"We must go . . . back to the . . . house!" Romara said. "We must get . . . away from here . . . immediately!"

"G-get—away?"

"This is Sir Harvey's doing. He is trying to steal Alexander from you. He wants him!"

"How—do you—know?" Caryl asked in a quivering voice.

"I will tell you everything, dearest, but now we must get away and hide somewhere."

"Why? Why?" Caryl asked.

"I will explain, I promise you, but we cannot stay here now."

As they walked quickly back to the house, Romara was frantically making plans in her mind.

One thing, it seemed to her, was obvious: Lord Ravenscar must not be involved any more than he was already.

Now Sir Harvey would not only have a charge to bring against his wife but also one against Romara.

The idea that she might have to stand trial for murder was terrifying; but if she could not be found, she could make it impossible for them to bring such a charge.

She felt almost sick at the thought of how humiliating it would be for Lord Ravenscar that his wife should stand in the dock at the Old Bailey.

She knew too that the fact that a man had died by her hand would be another weapon for Sir Harvey to use against Caryl in order to gain possession of his son.

Because she was so afraid, and at the same time because so much rested on what they now did, she felt almost as if she was given a calmness which was not natural but which made her think clearly and act decisively.

"Behave as if nothing has happened," she said to Caryl as they walked up the steps to the front door.

There was a footman on duty in the Hall and Romara said in quite an ordinary tone:

"Will you order the little pony-cart? Her Ladyship and I wish to go to the village to buy something and we do not want our picnic-luncheon removed until I give further orders."

"Very good, M'Lady."

Romara and Caryl hurried up the stairs. It was just after noon, which was the servants' luncheon-time. Mrs. Fellows and the housemaids were downstairs, and, because they were out, the Nurse would be with them.

Romara went into her bed-room, and, taking Alexander from Caryl, laid him on the bed.

"Go to the Nursery and fetch just a few things you think he will need," she said. "We can buy the rest."

Caryl looked at her wide-eyed, but she obeyed.

Then Romara pulled a small valise from the cupboard and filled it with several gowns that both she and Caryl could wear but which were the quietest and least ostentatious they possessed.

It was lucky that it was so hot, Romara thought, and they would not want many thick, heavy garments.

Two pretty shawls should keep them warm if necessary, and it was more important to have nightgowns and chemises than anything else.

She thrust everything into the valise; then, putting the shawls on the bed, she rushed to the writing-desk and scribbled a note to Lord Ravenscar.

A minute or so later Caryl came hurrying into the room, with her bonnet on her head, her arms full of Alexander's small garments.

Without saying anything, Romara discarded several of his more elaborate robes and pushed the rest on top of the other garments in the valise.

Then she picked it up and put on her bonnet, saying:

"Carry Alexander, and try to look as if we really are just going to the village."

"Have you any money?" Caryl asked.

"Fortunately, I have!" Romara answered. "I asked Mr. Arkwright for some last week, when I intended going to Beaconsfield to buy some things you needed, but in the end I did not go."

She paused, then added:

"I tell you what, bring your jewellery with you. We can sell it when we need more money."

Caryl ran obediently to fetch her jewellery.

There was nothing very valuable except for a

brooch which Sir Harvey had given her the first week they had run away together and a ring that she had worn secretly when he was still trying to persuade her to leave home and marry him.

It was poetic justice, Romara thought, that Sir Harvey's presents should be instrumental in keeping Caryl, Alexander, and Romara in hiding from him.

Romara knew, of course, that they could not exist forever on what they possessed, but she was quite certain that the most important thing was to go into hiding while the first "hue and cry" took place over the dead man.

Later, perhaps, she would be able to obtain some of her father's money.

His Solicitor was an elderly man whom Romara had known all her life, and she felt that if she appealed to him as a friend rather than a Legal Adviser he would help her secretly.

There was, however, no time to think very far ahead, and all Romara was certain of was that now they should get away as quickly as possible.

She and Caryl walked down the stairs and the footman waiting for them did not perceive the valise until she reached his side.

"Excuse me, M'Lady," he said, reaching out for it.

"Put it in the pony-cart," Romara said. "It is some material we are taking with us to match at the little shop."

She knew that the young man was not interested in the information but she hoped that he would remember it later.

The pony-cart was really intended for a child, and it was what Lord Ravenscar had driven when he was a small boy.

Romara had already taken Caryl for a drive in it when she was still not well enough to walk, and the groom who had brought it to the door now did not expect to accompany them.

"Thank you, Harris," Romara said with a smile. "We shall not be long."

Respectfully putting his fingers to his forehead,

he watched them with an admiring look in his eyes as they drove away.

"Where are we... going?" Caryl asked in a frightened voice.

"We are going onto the highway," Romara replied firmly. "We will drive for a few miles, where we will leave the pony-cart and take the Stage-Coach."

"Where to?" Caryl asked again.

Romara shook her head.

"I do not know," she answered. "Perhaps to some small village, very quiet, where no-one will think to look for us."

Caryl said nothing, she only held Alexander close against her. After they had driven a little way Romara began to tell her what was in the letter which had come for her a week ago.

They drove for nearly three miles before Romara realised that the pony was getting tired, and there was a small way-side Inn ahead where she decided she would leave the cart.

They drove into the yard.

An elderly ostler came to assist them.

"This pony and cart belongs to Lord Ravenscar," Romara said to him, "and I would be most grateful if you would return it to Raven House."

"Us be short-'anded, Ma'am," the man replied.

He was obviously in charge, and Romara drew a guinea from her purse.

"I am sure His Lordship will be only too pleased to pay you for this service."

At the sight of the money, the man was all smiles and affability.

"T'shall be done, Ma'am, make no mistake. T'shall be done as soon as th' pony's rested."

"Thank you very much," Romara answered.

She discovered what time the next Stage-Coach was expected, then took Caryl inside the Inn to sit down.

"You are feeling all right, dearest?" she asked.

"A little tired and very—frightened," Caryl replied.

"We will not go far tonight," Romara said, "but we must get away."

"Yes, of course. I understand," Caryl agreed.

"You are being very brave and helpful," Romara told her.

She thought in fact that Caryl was behaving very well, and it was only Sir Harvey's cruelty which had made her so helpless and tearful when they were in London.

Now, when she knew she was fighting for her son, she had an unexpected fortitude which was very touching.

Romara insisted that they both have a cup of tea and eat a plate of freshly cut ham.

It was not expensive, but Romara thought that from now on they would have to count every penny.

Although, as she had said, she had some money with her, it would certainly not last forever, and she had no desire to let anyone know their whereabouts for a long time.

She hoped that before they were penniless Sir Harvey would give up the thought of finding them and that even the Magistrates would think it was hopeless.

When it grew near to the time for the Stage-Coach to arrive, Romara and Caryl went outside the Inn and stood waiting.

There were several other people there already: a fat farmer's wife carrying a basket full of eggs, a man in a mole-skin coat who looked like a game-keeper, and two small, obstreperous boys whose mother had no control over them.

Caryl sat on the upturned valise with Alexander in her arms while Romara kept looking down the road, hoping at any moment to see the Stage-Coach, usually overloaded with passengers, coming towards them in a cloud of dust.

But the road was empty and everybody began to fidget and look at their watches.

Still there was no Stage-Coach.

Then at last there was a vehicle approaching, but

it turned out to be a two-horse Chaise driven by a gentleman wearing a tall hat.

He was going at quite a quick rate, but when he neared the Inn he slowed down his horses and drew up beside the small crowd of people, who were staring at him.

"Are you waiting for the Stage-Coach?" he asked.

"Aye, Sir," replied the man who looked like a game-keeper. "An' it's long overdue."

"I'm afraid you will have to wait a good deal longer," said the gentlemen in the Chaise. "There has been an accident. No-one was hurt, but it will take some time to get the coach out of the ditch and back onto the road."

"That would go an' 'appen!" the fat farmer's wife exclaimed. "An' me late already!"

The gentleman looked at Romara, then at Caryl with the small baby in her arms.

"Perhaps I could give you two ladies a lift?" he suggested.

Romara looked at him searchingly. She thought he had a kind and trustworthy face, and Caryl was obviously tired.

"That would be very kind," she replied.

The man in the mole-skin coat obliged by lifting their valise onto the back of the Chaise, then they climbed in.

Romara sat next to the driver so that Caryl would be more comfortable on the outside.

The gentleman started his horses off, then he said:

"Let me introduce myself. My name is Buxton, William Buxton, but most people where I live call me 'Squire.' "

It struck Romara as he spoke that she had not decided by what names she and Caryl should be known. With only a slight hesitation, she chose for herself her mother's name.

"My name is Lindsey," she said, "Miss Lindsey. And my sister is Mrs. Hammond."

"I am delighted to meet you!" Mr. Buxton said. "And where may I take you?"

There was a little pause before Romara answered:

"As it happens, my sister and I were looking for a quiet village where we could stay for a short holiday."

"A quiet village?" Mr. Buxton asked in surprise.

"She has not been well, and we thought the country air would be good for the baby."

"So you come from the town!"

"Yes," Romara agreed briefly.

Mr. Buxton did not speak and after a moment she said:

"Perhaps you could recommend somewhere... not expensive, of course."

"I was just thinking," he said, "that the Inn in the village near my house does not take guests, but I am sure I could get you put up at my Home Farm, if that would suit you."

"It sounds delightful!" Romara replied.

"The farmer's wife, Mrs. Coswell, is very fond of babies. In fact she is always telling me that the farm is too big for her now that her children are grown up and married."

"A farm is just what I would like for my sister and her baby son," Romara said quickly.

"Then that is where I will take you," Mr. Buxton said. "We have not far to go. The village of Little Bowbrook is only about two miles away."

It was, Romara thought, the sort of village one read about in books. There was an Inn on the village green, a few thatched cottages, and a small grey-stone Church.

They drove through some gates flanked by two small lodges and travelled down a tree-bordered drive which led, Mr. Buxton said, to his own house.

They caught a glimpse of it before Mr. Buxton turned the horses' heads to go along a rather rough track which led to the farm.

It was a long, low, red-brick building surrounded

by sheds and cow-stalls, with a number of fat ducks fluttering out of the way of the horses as they approached the front door.

Mrs. Coswell, a grey-haired woman, greeted Mr. Buxton effusively.

"Oi thinks it were yer horses, Squire, a-coming into the yard," she said. " 'Tis nice to see ye again so soon."

"I have brought you two paying guests, Mrs. Coswell," Mr. Buxton announced. "These ladies are looking for somewhere quiet for their holiday, and I could think of nowhere where they could be more comfortable than with you."

"That's real kind of ye, Squire, an' I'd love to have 'em," Mrs. Coswell replied.

Then she saw Alexander and gave an exclamation of delight.

"What a fine baby! Now ye give 'im to Oi while ye step out. Oi'll be careful o' 'im, having held six o' me own an' three grandchildren in me arms."

She rocked Alexander against her fat bosom, looking down at him with an expression on her face that was very maternal.

A boy appeared seemingly from nowhere to go to the horses' heads.

"I'll carry in your valise for you," Mr. Buxton said to Romara.

"You are very kind," she said. "Thank you very much."

Mrs. Coswell turned from her contemplation of Alexander to see what was happening.

"Now ye put tha' right doon, Squire," she ordered. "Mr. Coswell'll be home in a short while an' he'll take it upstairs for the ladies. Ye come right in an' 'ave a cup o' tay. It won't take Oi a minute t' bring it into th' Parlour."

Mrs. Coswell like a mother-hen shooed them all into a small Parlour which was obviously not often used.

It was, however, a comfortable room despite the stiffness of the chairs and the hardness of the sofa.

"You'll be all right here," Mr. Buxton said.

He appeared to be speaking to Romara, but his eyes were on Caryl.

"I think it is exactly what we were looking for," Romara agreed.

Mrs. Coswell came in to lay the table and pile it with so much food that Romara was certain that if they stayed long at the farm they would be as fat as their hostess.

There was a home-made loaf hot from the oven. There were scones and pasties, slices of home-cured ham, and an ox-tongue that Mrs. Coswell assured them she had boiled only the day before.

There were huge pats of golden butter and a jug of Jersey milk that was as thick as cream. There was also a comb of honey from the farmer's own bees and a pot of jam which Mrs. Coswell had made herself when the strawberries were ripe.

"It is delicious!" Caryl said. "Do you have all these delectable things in your house, Mr. Buxton?"

"The farm provides me with everything I need," Mr. Buxton answered, "and I sell the rest."

"Have you a large herd of cows?" Romara enquired.

"About a hundred," he answered. "I farm a thousand acres and I own another five thousand."

He gave a rather rueful laugh.

"It sounds as if I am boasting, but you did ask me."

"I love farms," Caryl said dreamily. "I like the cluck of the chickens, the quack of the ducks, and the moo of the cows when they are coming home for milking."

"Will you allow me to show you my herd tomorrow?" Mr. Buxton asked.

"Yes, please," Caryl answered. "Have you any calves?"

"Masses of them!"

"And you will not forget to show them to me?"

"I promise you I shall not forget that," he answered.

Romara thought with a smile that Caryl had made a conquest.

She was not surprised, for her sister looked very pretty with her fair hair showing under her straw bonnet and the blue ribbons enhancing the pink-and-white clarity of her skin.

In her heart she said a little prayer of thankfulness that they had been so fortunate as to find Mr. Buxton and he had been kind enough to bring them to his farm.

It was not only comfortable, but she was quite certain that it was safe.

And who would suspect two holiday-makers of having important names and one of them being a murderess?

She felt herself shiver as she thought of it.

Then she had a sudden longing for Lord Ravenscar, which swept over her almost like a tidal wave.

Only if he was there could she feel really safe.

Only if she could hold on to him would she not feel that terrifying fear in her heart that both she and Caryl were in deadly danger.

Chapter Six

"We will be back before tea," Caryl said, "and I am looking forward to my Birthday-cake."

"You are not supposed to know you are having one!" Romara answered. "And do not be late."

"No, of course not," Caryl replied as she moved towards the farm-house door.

She stopped and said:

"Would you like to come with us, Romara?"

Her sister shook her head.

"I have no wish to play 'gooseberry' to you and the Squire."

"You would never be that, dearest," Caryl answered, and added with a little smile: "At the same time, I do like having him on my own!"

Romara understood, although her heart was heavy as she watched Caryl drive away in the Chaise beside Mr. Buxton.

What would be the end of it?

Caryl had quite obviously been in love with the Squire, as everybody called him, for weeks, and he with her. But last night she had come into Romara's bed-room after they had retired to sit on her bed and say:

"I have something to tell you, Romara, and it may make you angry."

"It would be very difficult for me to be angry with you," Romara replied.

"I hope you will—forgive me," Caryl answered, "but I have told William who I—am."

She spoke hesitatingly and looked apprehensively at her sister as if she expected her to be furious with her.

"I anticipated that you would do that," Romara replied.

"Of course I did not tell him about you—that would have been disloyal. But he—had to know the—truth."

There was a little pause and then Romara asked:

"Are you going to tell me why?"

"I think you know the answer to that. He loves me! He loves me and wants to marry me!"

Caryl clasped her hands together in anguish and said:

"And I want it more than anything in the world, but how can I ever be free? Oh! Romara, how can I be free?"

Romara reached out to put her arms round her sister.

"I wish I could answer that," she said after a moment, and her eyes were full of tears.

What Caryl had told her was not unexpected. It was quite obvious that ever since they had come to live on the farm, the Squire had eyes for no-one else.

He called every day and took them driving, sometimes to see his home.

This was a delightful old Manor which had been in the Buxton family for generations and had been added on to and improved until it was, Romara thought, the perfect type of small country house that any woman would love.

It was very easy to imagine Caryl in the attractive Drawing-Room with its Queen Anne walnut furniture and rose-patterned chinzes—or sitting in the oval Dining-Room with its ancient fireplace and the portraits of the Squire's ancestors on the walls.

What was more important than the house was that he was exactly the type of husband whom Caryl should have.

He was quiet, considerate, gentle, and at the same time authoritative in a way that made one respect him as a man and made all those whom he employed look up to him with admiration.

Romara had learnt a lot about the Squire from the Coswells, who adored him, and she had found herself wishing over and over again that Caryl had met William Buxton before she had been seduced and made utterly miserably by Sir Harvey.

"But if wishes could come true," she told herself severely, "I would find . . . happiness!"

Every day during the five weeks they had been at the farm she had not only thought about Lord Ravenscar but had yearned for him in a manner that at times made her cry helplessly into her pillow.

It was no use telling herself that her longing for him, and what she knew, if she was honest, was her love, was quite hopeless.

She must hide away for his sake, so that he would never find her; but even if he did find her, she knew, he loved someone else.

The thought of Atalie Bray and her beauty seemed to haunt Romara to such an extent that when she looked into the mirror she did not see her own face but the face, as she imagined it, of Atalie Bray.

How, she asked herself, could she have been so foolish, so stupid, as to fall in love with a man who could never feel for her anything but disgust because he had married her in such a wild, irresponsible manner?

"It was . . . inevitable that I should . . . fall in love with him," Romara whispered to herself.

She shut her eyes and could see his strong, handsome face; his eyes looking searchingly at hers; his firm chin and mouth, which often twisted cynically.

"I love him! I love him!" she cried in the darkness.

Despairingly she thought sometimes that the only way she could serve him would be to die.

Then he would be free and there would no longer

be the question of finding her to see her stand trial for the murder she had committed.

However unhappy her thoughts might be, it was difficult in the daytime not to be grateful for the haven of quietness which, by an exceedingly lucky chance, she and Caryl had found.

If the Stage-Coach had not had an accident; if Mr. Buxton had not stopped to tell those waiting for it that it would be still longer delayed; if he had not offered Caryl and her a lift—where might they be to-day?

It was so like him, his consideration for other people, to have reassured the wayside passengers, and if they had searched the whole of England it would have been difficult to find a lodging as comfortable and as inexpensive as the Home Farm.

Romara felt ashamed when she paid Mrs. Coswell the minute sum that she asked every week for their keep.

She was sure that the Squire had told Mrs. Coswell not to be grasping, but it would have been foreign to the farmer's wife to be anything but hospitable and generous.

She looked after Alexander as if he were one of her own children, and because she thought it was too much for Caryl to feed him she had found a Wet-Nurse.

One of her daughters-in-law who had just given birth to a baby girl was only too willing to wet-nurse another child.

Without Alexander draining her strength, and with the Squire looking at her with admiration and tenderness, Caryl blossomed like a flower.

The food on the farm was delicious and the tension went from her face and the lines disappeared from under her eyes.

She looked, Romara thought, as if she were eighteen again, and there was no Sir Harvey knocking on the door to turn her from a lovely, light-hearted young girl into a miserable, frightened woman.

It was only right, Romara had thought last night

after Caryl had left her, that Mr. Buxton should know what he was up against.

In his company Caryl might find it easier to forget Sir Harvey and his threats.

Romara felt certain that he would still want to possess his son and that he would not give up the chase so easily.

When they had first come to the farm, every time there was the sound of wheels driving into the yard, or a knock at the door, she would hold her breath.

She would feel terrified in case it was one of Sir Harvey's men coming to demand the return of Alexander, or a Police Officer ordering her to appear in front of the Magistrates.

But gradually the good food, the rest, and the comforting attentions of Mrs. Coswell dulled Romara's fear, although nothing could prevent her heart from crying out for Lord Ravenscar.

She tortured herself with the thought that he must have gone back to London and forgotten her very existence amongst his friends at Carlton House and in the House of Lords.

Why should he give even a thought to the woman who bore his name and who had disappeared out of his life as swiftly as she had come into it?

"Think of me! Think of me!" Romara would whisper sometimes.

She felt as if she sent her thoughts on wings, searching for him, trying to find him wherever he might be.

But her mind told her that he would have forgotten and she would just be an ugly memory which would gradually erase itself as his life continued on an even keel.

Now, having watched Caryl and the Squire almost out of sight, Romara walked into the big kitchen where Mrs. Coswell was icing the Birthday-cake that she had made for Caryl's nineteenth Birthday.

She was applying the icing sugar with a bunch of goose feathers as Romara had seen the housewives in Huntingdonshire do and the result was certainly very attractive.

As she walked to the kitchen-table she said:

"My sister will be thrilled. She has always loved her Birthday-cakes ever since she was a small child."

"One never grows t' old for 'em," Mrs. Coswell said. "Although Squire laughed at Oi last year when Oi baked 'im one."

"I expect he ate it all the same," Romara said with a smile.

"That 'e did!" Mrs. Coswell said. "Would ye fancy a hot bun, dearie? Oi've a batch in th' oven."

"No, please do not tempt me!" Romara cried. "I am getting so fat on all your delicious food that I am having to let out my own gowns as well as Caryl's."

"An' about time where ye' sister be concerned," Mrs. Coswell said. "As Oi've told 'er often 'nough, she's a figure like a broom-stick!"

She stood back for a moment to admire her handiwork, and added:

"Not that Squire'd care if 'er be as stout as Oi be!"

Romara said nothing, as she knew only too well that Mrs. Coswell was exceedingly curious to learn if Caryl was a widow or had a husband somewhere in the world.

They were always very careful to say nothing in front of her which would answer the questions they knew trembled on her lips.

"We must be careful! We must be very, very careful," Romara had said over and over again to Caryl.

She told herself she was glad that their secret was now known to Squire, as undoubtedly it would make him more careful as to where he took Caryl.

She had always been afraid that they might drive off his estate and be seen by men who might be looking for her.

Today, she knew, they were only going for a short drive to look at the Squire's herds and therefore it was quite unnecessary for her to be nervous.

"Ye be a-looking serious, dearie," Mrs. Coswell said. "Enjoy yerself while ye be young, that's what Oi always says. Worry comes wi' old age!"

"If I am as little worried as you are when I get

older," Romara replied, "I shall be a very happy person!"

"Oi be 'appy 'cause Oi've a fine 'usband an' Oi thanks God for 'im every day," Mrs. Coswell said. "There's never a woman who 'as 'ad a better 'usband than Mr. Coswell."

"I am sure of that," Romara agreed.

Jake Coswell was a somewhat inarticulate man, but there was no doubt that he loved his wife and his family as well as he loved the land he farmed and the animals he looked after.

Every morning of his life he rose before five o'clock.

The reason the Home Farm was a thriving success was that he personally attended to everything and saw that the men under him took the same interest in their work as he did.

"The Squire is lucky to have him," Romara told herself.

She found herself thinking of the day she and Lord Ravenscar had visited the Westons.

Mrs. Weston had wished her every happiness and had told Lord Ravenscar he was fortunate to have such a lovely wife!

She supposed they and the other farmers she had visited on the estate would be wondering what had happened to her.

But perhaps they knew of what had occurred and thought of her with horror and as unworthy of the Master they served.

Romara walked across the flagged floor of the big kitchen to stand at the door, looking at the ducks and geese drinking in the small pond outside and listening to the chickens clucking amongst the straw in the barn.

The peace of it made her wonder if she had really been involved in such dramatic incidents.

Could she have been knocked unconscious by Sir Harvey? Married by a drunken Parson? Killed a man who was trying to kidnap Caryl's baby?

It all seemed impossible!

Because her thoughts made her restless and unhappy she left Mrs. Coswell in the kitchen and went into the Parlour to pick up her sewing.

There was always a lot of mending to do because they had so few things with them.

Unable themselves to go to the shops, Romara had asked Mrs. Coswell on market-day to bring back a roll of muslin, out of which she had made pretty, fresh dresses for Caryl and herself.

They certainly could not vie with the expensive gowns Sir Harvey had given Caryl, but those were certainly not suitable for the country.

Soon Alexander would have grown out of everything he possessed, even though Romara had let out his long gowns.

'We shall soon need more money,' she thought in a sudden panic.

It would be humiliating to have to ask the Squire for a loan, and she wondered whether it would be safe for her to go to London to see her father's solicitor.

'I will discuss it with Caryl,' she thought.

Then she knew that Caryl would think it absurd of her not to accept anything that the Squire would be only too willing to give them.

"What will be the end?"

"What will happen?"

"How can we go on forever like this?"

The questions turned over and over in Romara's mind.

At last she heard the sound of horses' hoofs and knew that Caryl had returned.

Her sister's eyes were shining and her lips were smiling, and Romara had the idea that she had been kissed.

It was reprehensible, it was wrong, when she was a married woman, but who could expect any woman to be loyal to a man as loathsome as Sir Harvey Wychbold?

"We are back! You see we are back!" Caryl cried with a lilt in her voice as her sister appeared in the doorway.

"Have you had a nice drive?" Romara asked.

"Wonderful!" Caryl exclaimed rapturously. "And look what William has given me as a Birthday-present."

She held up her arm as she spoke and Romara saw that round her wrist there was a gold bracelet set with turquoises and diamonds.

"Is it not lovely!" Caryl exclaimed.

She looked up at her sister and knew by her expression that she did not approve.

"It is no use, dearest," she whispered. "He so much wanted to give me a present, and who will know except you?"

"No . . . I suppose it is . . . all right," Romara murmured.

She could not help thinking that Caryl was drifting away on a dangerous current, but she had no wish to spoil the happiness of her Birthday.

The Squire had handed over his horses to the care of the farm-boy and now he came into the small Hall to ask:

"Is tea ready? Caryl was most insistent that we should not be late!"

"I am sure it is," Romara replied, "but wait a moment while I go and see."

It was only a few steps to the kitchen, and she opened the door and put her head round it to ask:

"They are back, Mrs. Coswell. Shall I bring them in?"

"Oi just 'ave to light th' last three candles," Mrs. Coswell replied.

Romara saw that while Mrs. Coswell was performing this task, her husband had come in early to take part in the ceremonial cutting of the cake and to eat a slice of it.

Afterwards they would have tea in the Parlour, but it was Romara who arranged that Mrs. Coswell, who had taken so much trouble, should see them cut the cake.

Her daughter-in-law was in the corner of the kitchen, nursing Alexander in her arms.

Romara waited a moment, saw the last candle flicker into life, and then opened the kitchen door.

"Come in," she called.

She saw as she turned her head that Caryl was looking up at the Squire and they were whispering to each other as people do when they are in love.

She felt her heart contract at the happy picture they made, and though she tried to prevent it a little sharp stab of envy struck through her heart almost like a dagger.

There was only one man she would like to look at her like that. One man she would like to be here at this moment.

But what was the point of thinking about it?

Caryl moved somewhat guiltily away from the Squire's side and walked towards Romara.

"Now for the surprise!" She smiled and led them into the kitchen.

The cake was, expectedly, a very large one, as Mrs. Coswell judged everything by her own size!

Romara knew that pounds of sultanas, currants, cherries, and walnuts had gone into the making of it. Then it had been covered with an inch-thick marzipan and finally with white-and-pink icing which was very like Caryl's complexion.

With nineteen candles burning on it, it was certainly very impressive, and Caryl gave a cry of delight and clapped her hands.

"It is magnificent! The grandest cake I have ever had!" she exclaimed. "Thank you! Thank you, Mrs. Coswell!"

"I am glad you like it, Ma'am," Mrs. Coswell said, very gratified.

She always remembered Caryl's married status and addressed her as "Ma'am." But because she looked on Romara as merely an unmarried girl, she often forgot to be formal.

"Now, Jake," Mrs. Coswell said sharply to her husband, "ye've not seen Mrs. 'ammond afore terday, so give 'er yer wishes!"

" 'Appy Birthday, Ma'am," Jake muttered uncomfortably.

"Thank you! Thank you for everything!" Caryl replied. "And now I must cut it."

"'Twill be a bit stiff," Mrs. Coswell said, taking up a large knife. "Ye 'ad better give 'er a 'and, Squire. Th' cake be one of th' richest Oi've ever made."

"Then we will undoubtedly all have indigestion," Mr. Buxton said with a smile. "It took me a long time to recover from your Christmas-cake!"

"Get on wi' ye!" Mrs. Coswell exclaimed. "Ye be as good as a trenchman as ye've been since ye were a small boy an' as noisy as Alexander when ye were 'ungry!"

They all laughed at this, and Caryl said to Mrs. Coswell's daughter-in-law:

"Do bring Alexander nearer so he can see the pretty candles."

The baby was duly propped up in his Nurse's arms and Caryl looked at him with an adoring expression on her face.

"I think he is trying to reach out towards them! Do look, Romara, he loves the pretty lights!"

"We are waiting for you to cut the cake, dearest," Romara said with a smile.

"Yes, of course!" Caryl said.

She took the knife and thrust it into the icing, but as the blade came into contact with the heavy cake Caryl glanced up at the Squire, giving him a wordless invitation to assist her.

His firm hand covered hers and there was an expression in his eyes as he touched Caryl which Romara thought was very revealing.

Then as they pressed the knife through the cake Romara cried:

"Do not forget to make a wish for what you want most to happen this coming year."

As she spoke she had no doubt that Caryl and the Squire were both making the same wish, and she saw that they moved a little closer to each other.

Then as the knife slid to the bottom of the cake there was a noise of heavy footsteps unexpectedly coming through the open kitchen door.

Romara turned her head to see a flamboyantly red face and an overpowering and overdressed figure.

It was impossible for her to move, impossible too for her to cry out a warning!

Only as Caryl and the Squire jointly pulled the knife from the cake did Caryl's eyes rise, and she gave a sudden cry.

"Harvey!"

Her voice was low but somehow it seemed to vibrate round the kitchen.

"Yes, Harvey," he replied. "And no doubt you are surprised to see me. But you could not really have been such a fool as to think you could escape me forever."

Caryl did not answer. Her voice, like Romara's, seemed to be strangled in her throat.

She could only stand there staring wide-eyed at her husband, and the knife fell from her hand with a clatter onto the table.

"Charming little family party!" Sir Harvey sneered. "And I see my son is also present."

His eyes rested for a moment on the baby, who still appeared to be looking at the bright lights, and instantly Caryl took a step towards Alexander.

"You shall not have him!" she said fiercely. "You shall not take him away from me!"

"That is a silly and idiotic statement, to which I will pay no attention," Sir Harvey said. "You either come with the child as I have ordered you to do, or I will take him with me!"

"No! No!" Caryl cried.

Back in her voice was the terror which Romara had heard before when she was with her in Curzon Street.

Mr. Buxton stepped round the side of the table.

"Now look here, Sir," he said, "I would like to discuss this matter with you."

"Who the hell are you?" Sir Harvey enquired.

"A friend of your wife," the Squire replied. "I think the best thing would be for us to go into another room where we can talk this matter over in private."

"I have nothing to say to you!" Sir Harvey retorted. "Although you call yourself my wife's friend, I imagine you are in fact her lover!"

"I am nothing of the sort," the Squire contradicted sharply, "and you have no right to cast such aspersions on her!"

Sir Harvey laughed and it was not a pleasant sound.

"My wife's good name is a matter of conjecture," he said. "You can keep her if you want her. All I am interested in is my child."

"You shall not have him! You shall not!" Caryl cried. "He is mine! You never wanted him and I will never give him up!"

The tears were running down Caryl's face as Romara walked towards Sir Harvey.

"Please do not upset Caryl," she said in a low voice. "She was in a weak state when I brought her away from London and she must not be upset again."

"So you are interfering again, are you!" Sir Harvey said in an ugly tone. "Do you want me to treat you as I treated you last time? Make no mistake about it, I shall not hesitate to do so!"

There was something so ferocious in the way he spoke that instinctively Romara took a step backwards, holding on to a chair near the window as if to stop herself from falling.

Sir Harvey laughed again unpleasantly.

"Make your mind up," he said to Caryl. "Are you coming with the child, or am I taking him alone?"

"You will do neither," Mr. Buxton said in a quiet voice. "I dare say you have certain rights, but I have already suggested we talk this over quietly and without heat."

As he spoke he moved in front of Caryl as if to protect her.

"How dare you try to interfere between me and my wife!" Sir Harvey shouted.

Now he was crimson in the face, the way he had been before, when he had come raging into his Sitting-Room in Curzon Street.

"I understand," the Squire said, "that you are

trying to prove that your wife is not a fit and proper person to have the care of her child. But I, Sir Harvey, do not consider you fit or proper to look after either your wife or your son!"

His words seemed for a moment to take Sir Harvey's breath away. Then suddenly he put his hand into the pocket of his driving-coat and brought out a pistol.

He pointed it at the Squire and said angrily:

"Get out of my way! Caryl, come here and bring me that child!"

"No! No!" Caryl screamed. "He is mine! Mine! Not yours!"

"Your behaviour is outrageous!" the Squire said.

Sir Harvey did not answer, he only glared at the man confronting him, and Romara saw his finger tighten on the trigger.

Without stopping to think or to scream, she ran forwards and just as Sir Harvey fired at the Squire she tried to force his arm upwards.

He was too strong for her, but the bullet instead of striking the Squire in the heart, where Sir Harvey had aimed, only grazed his arm, cutting through his coat to bury itself in the wall behind him, shattering some of the white plaster, which fell onto the floor.

The sound of the report echoed and re-echoed round the kitchen and Sir Harvey brought down the pistol to fire again.

But before he could do so Mr. Buxton drew a pistol from his pocket and shot Sir Harvey straight in the chest.

For a moment it seemed as if the shot made no impact on him. Then slowly, so slowly that it was terrifying to watch, he subsided to his knees and then fell, still slowly, but heavily, onto the floor.

His mouth was open and so were his eyes, but Romara could look only at Caryl. She was holding on to the Squire, crying frantically over and over again:

"He might have—killed you! He—might have—killed you!"

It was then that Romara heard the sound of wheels outside the kitchen door.

Almost without realising what she was doing, she looked to see who was arriving.

With a little sound which seemed to be strangled in her throat she ran out the door and into the yard.

The man who was descending from the Phaeton had only just reached the ground when she flung herself against him.

"You have . . . come!" she said, "Oh! Thank . . . God! I have . . . wanted . . . you! I have . . . wanted you so . . . desperately!"

She was hanging on to the lapels of his coat with both hands and her face was upturned to his.

Lord Ravenscar looked down at her and asked angrily:

"How could you disappear in that damnable fashion?"

Then his arms went round her and his lips came down on hers.

Romara found it impossible to move, impossible to breathe, and then almost before she could realise what had happened he had set her aside.

"What the hell is going on?" he asked, and walked into the kitchen.

The body of Sir Harvey was lying directly in front of him and he glanced at it before he saw Caryl with her arms round the Squire, who had one arm hanging at his side, with blood already running over his hand.

Everyone else seemed to be staring, white-faced, from the other side of the table on which the nineteen candles were still burning brightly on the iced cake.

For a moment no-one spoke, and then with a note of surprise in his voice the Squire exclaimed:

"Hullo, Trent! This is an unexpected visit and you have come at a somewhat unfortunate moment!"

"Not unexpected!" Lord Ravenscar said savagely. "I have been following that swine all the way from London. But I see, William, that you have disposed of him very effectively!"

"He shot at me first," Mr. Buxton answered, "and he had no idea I was armed!"

"Just the sort of thing he would do," Lord Ravenscar said scathingly.

"Mr. Buxton fired in . . . self-defence," Romara said breathlessly.

"His pistol has two chambers in it," the Squire added. "If he had fired again as he intended, he would have undoubtedly killed me. But Romara saved my life."

Lord Ravenscar looked at Romara and smiled.

"That does not surprise me," he said.

" 'Twere self-defence, Sir," Farmer Coswell said slowly, as if he had just caught up with the conversation.

"Indeed 'twas!" Mrs. Coswell chimed in. "Oi couldn't believe me eyes. E'd 'ave murdered our Squire if it'd not been for th' young lady."

"You see I have my witnesses," the Squire remarked to Lord Ravenscar.

Then he looked down at Caryl, who was sobbing helplessly on his shoulder.

"It is all right, darling," he said, as if no-one else was present. "It is all over, he is dead!"

"You have—killed him to—prevent him taking Alexander—away from me," Caryl sobbed, "but—will it mean—trouble for—you?"

"There will be no trouble, I promise you! Everything can be explained," the Squire said tenderly.

Lord Ravenscar listened to this exchange with some surprise. Then as if in his usual manner he was ready to take charge he said:

"The best thing we can do, William, is for you and me and this man, who witnessed what occurred, to go at once to see the Chief Constable. Fortunately, he is a friend of us both."

"Yes, that is what we had better do," the Squire agreed.

Lord Ravenscar made a contemptuous gesture towards the prostrate body of Sir Harvey, and, speaking to Farmer Coswell, said:

"Before we leave you had better remove this carrion from your kitchen. Put it out of sight until we send a Parson to bury him."

As if Farmer Coswell understood the voice of authority, he touched his forelock, murmuring:

"Oi'll do that, Sir."

Lord Ravenscar looked at Romara.

"You and Caryl pack," he said, "and as soon as Buxton and I return, I will take you home."

Romara looked at him wide-eyed.

"They . . . they . . . are not . . . looking for me?"

A faint smile twisted Lord Ravenscar's lips.

"You overestimated your skill with a pistol. If you shot to kill, you were somewhat wide of the mark."

"He . . . is not . . . dead?"

Romara could hardly believe the words.

Lord Ravenscar shook his head.

"He is undoubtedly extremely uncomfortable," he replied. "But your bull's-eye, my little Amazon, was in the shoulder!"

For a moment Romara could hardly believe she had heard him aright. Then almost blindly she put out her hands towards Lord Ravenscar, saying weakly:

"I . . . cannot . . . believe it. I . . . think I am . . . going to . . . faint."

He put his arm round her to support her as he said briskly:

"Nonsense! You have got to get your packing done, and William and I will not be long. The Chief Constable lives only about two miles away."

"I thought he . . . would be . . . looking for . . . me," Romara whispered.

"We will talk about that when we get home," Lord Ravenscar replied.

Caryl raised her head from the Squire's shoulder.

"If Alexander and I are going back to Raven House," she said, "what about William?"

"William, whom I have known since I was your son's age, is, as he well knows, always welcome," Lord Ravenscar replied.

Caryl turned up her face eagerly towards the Squire.

"Come with us, please come with us!" she pleaded.

"I have every intention of doing so," he answered.

"But first go and do your packing as Trent suggests."

"Ye not be a-going anywhere, Squire," Mrs. Coswell interrupted, " 'til Oi've dressed yer arm!"

"It is only a scratch," Mr. Buxton protested.

But Mrs. Coswell had pulled off his jacket, and Caryl was exclaiming tearfully at the amount of blood there was on his shirt, before he could protest further.

It was in fact only a surface wound, and when Mrs. Coswell had bound it up deftly, he was ready to leave with Lord Ravenscar in his Phaeton to see the Chief Constable.

In the meantime, Farmer Coswell had dragged Sir Harvey's body away and Romara could not help thinking that although it was horrible for anyone to die, no-one would mourn him.

Now Caryl could marry the Squire, and Alexander, when he grew older, would never know what an unpleasant creature had fathered him.

In some magical way it all seemed as if the dark clouds that had been depressing her had swept away to reveal sunshine.

Her heart was beating quickly and excitedly because Lord Ravenscar was here and he was even better-looking and more impressive than she had remembered.

It seemed impossible to think that he had actually kissed her when he arrived.

But it was not really a kiss, she told herself, just a touch of his lips on hers when she was clinging to him because she had been so overwhelmingly glad to see him.

'I love him,' she thought, 'and now that he is here, everything seems different.'

As if he felt that she was thinking of him, Lord Ravenscar, who had been waiting almost impatiently while the Squire's arm was bandaged, turned his head to look at her.

She felt a little shy under the scrutiny of his eyes.

"How . . . did you find . . . me?"

"You may well ask!" he replied. "How could I

guess that you would be such a short distance away and with one of my oldest friends."

"I thought we . . . both had to . . . hide . . . somewhere, where . . . no-one would . . . find us."

Lord Ravenscar's lips tightened for a moment as if, she thought unhappily, in anger. Then he said:

"I knew Wychbold would never give up his pursuit of Caryl, so instead of sending out Bow Street Runners to look for you, I merely bribed his servants, as I have done before, to discover what information his men had obtained."

"That was . . . clever of you," Romara said admiringly.

"They told him first thing this morning that Caryl had been located staying on this farm. I received the information very few minutes after Wychbold had paid for it!"

"So you . . . followed him."

"And a rotten driver he is! 'Cow-fisted' my groom called him, and it was the right description!"

He had come at just the right moment, exactly when she had wanted him, Romara thought.

Then, because she longed to ask him if he had been anxious to find her, she bit the words back from her lips and put her arms round Caryl, saying:

"We had better go and do our packing, as His Lordship has ordered us to do."

Caryl paid no attention to her; she was looking up at the Squire.

"You will not be . . . long?" she whispered.

"I have to clear my name," he answered, "and then I will be back, I promise you."

As he spoke he lifted Caryl's hand to his lips and Romara heard him whisper very softly:

"Take care of yourself, my darling."

Then Lord Ravenscar and the Squire were driving away in the former's Phaeton, followed by Farmer Coswell in Mr. Buxton's Chaise.

"Never did Oi see th' likes in all me born days!" Mrs. Coswell exclaimed.

As she spoke Alexander began to wail.

"'E be hungry, that's what 'e be!" his wet-nurse said.

"And 'e'll be hungrier still," Mrs. Coswell retorted "if ye don't go wi' 'im to stay at Raven 'ouse."

"Stay at Raven 'ouse!" Her daughter-in-law gasped. "Whatever made ye think o' that?"

"Someone 'as to 'ave a 'ead on 'er shoulders," Mrs. Coswell snapped. "'Ow do ye think th' baby be a-going t' manage without ye?"

"Ye mean Oi'm t' stay wi' 'im at Raven 'ouse?"

"That's what Oi said," Mrs. Coswell replied.

"And take me own baby wi' Oi?"

"She'll 'ave t' go, o' course," Mrs. Coswell answered.

"What about Joe?"

"What do ye mean, what about Joe?" Mrs. Coswell questioned. "Oi've looked after me son for nigh on twenty-five years afore ye married 'im, so ye can trust Oi now!"

Her daughter-in-law smiled.

"Oi'm not a-saying that Oi wouldn't like t' see Raven 'ouse, but seems presumptuous me a-going there."

"An' what'd Alexander do without ye, ask yerself," Mrs. Coswell said. "G'on girl, get ready! Ye'll want a change o' clothing, an' take yer best dress, for ye'll be among all those gran' servants."

"Oi never expected, not in all me born days, t' be staying at Raven 'ouse," the daughter-in-law was muttering as she hurried upstairs to the room she occupied with her husband and her small daughter.

On the same floor, Caryl had her arms round Romara's neck, hugging her.

"I can marry William!" she was saying over and over again. "I can marry William! Oh! Romara, life is wonderful!"

"Hardly the right expression to come from a widow of less than half-an-hour," Romara teased. "But I am so glad, dearest. I am really."

"He is so kind, so understanding, and we will

live in that adorable house and I hope I have lots of babies to play with Alexander."

It all seemed like a fairy-tale with a happy ending, Romara thought, but throbbing in her mind and beating in her heart over and over again with every breath she drew was the question:

"What about me? What about me?"

It seemed to ring deafeningly in her ears all the time she was packing their box. Caryl was too excited to do anything except change into a fresh gown and look at herself in the mirror.

"Thank goodness!" she exclaimed. "When we get back to Raven House I can wear the pretty clothes I brought from London."

She gave a little cry of excitement.

"And buy new ones! Oh! Romara, do you realise I can have new gowns for my trousseau—if we can—afford them?"

"Of course we can afford a trousseau," Romara said with a smile.

Caryl looked at the bracelet she wore on her wrist.

"William said turquoises would bring me luck. He said that is what they believe in the East, and think how lucky I have been already!"

"You are very fortunate," Romara said. "And who would have expected the Squire to be a friend of . . . Lord Ravenscar?"

She paused because she could not bring herself to say "my husband."

"After all," Caryl said, "since they live in the same County and not far from each other, it might have been expected."

She smiled before she continued:

"I have often longed to ask William if he had ever been to Raven House. Then I thought perhaps he might have connected us with His Lordship and you would have been angry."

Romara sat back on her heels beside the trunk she was packing.

"I still cannot believe that I did not . . . kill that

man. I meant to, because he was taking away Alexander. I was sure I had . . . succeeded."

"It is a very good thing you did not!" Caryl replied. "If you had, it would have spoilt my wedding to have to come and tell you all about it while you were in prison!"

She was teasing but to Romara it was not really a laughing matter.

She had lain awake so often at night shivering because she might be brought to trial and convicted, if not to be charged then to be "confined at His Majesty's pleasure"!

Caryl saw Romara's face in the mirror and turned to put her arms round her and kiss her cheek.

"We will not think about it any more," she said. "You have been so brave and so wonderful to me that I can never be grateful enough. If it had not been for you, Alexander would not have had a name, or perhaps he would not have been born at all. Harvey never wanted him."

"If I have to forget, you have to forget too," Romara said. "I was thinking only this morning that you look as you used to look before Sir Harvey came into your life."

She paused before she went on:

"Go back to that time, Caryl. Forget this horrible, frightening experience and just be happy with William, who really loves you."

"I keep asking myself if what I felt for Harvey was love," Caryl said quietly, "but I now know that I was just infatuated because he was so plausible, so smart, and seemed to come from another world."

"You were too young to realise how awful he was," Romara said sympathetically.

"It is all like a nightmare," Caryl said, "but you are right, Romara—I will not think of him again, but only of William and how I can make him happy."

"I am sure you will do that." Romara smiled. "And you know, Caryl, that Papa would have liked William. He was just the sort of son-in-law he would have wanted."

"Lord Ravenscar is too."

Her sister did not answer and after a moment she said tentatively:

"I do not want to hurt you, but do you think he has . . . forgotten that woman who . . . jilted him?"

"I have no idea."

"I saw her once."

"You saw her!" Romara exclaimed. "Why did you not tell me?"

"I thought it might upset you," Caryl answered simply. "It was when I was at Vauxhall Gardens with Harvey. She was in the next box and he kept looking at her and saying how beautiful she was, to make me jealous."

She paused, then went on:

"I hated her! And I do not think she was a nice person."

"Why do you say that?" Romara asked.

"She was flirting with two or three men at the same time. Although she was deliberately exciting them, and they were obviously all thrilled, I could see that she did not care a jot for any of them."

Romara sighed. If that was the sort of person Lord Ravenscar liked, how could she possibly compete?

She knew she would never be good at flirting with one man, let alone three!

She was quite sure that even if they came to some sensible arrangement of living as man and wife, he would find her dull and doubtless would leave her alone in the country while he went to London to be with his friends.

"We must get on with our packing," she said abruptly.

"Yes, of course," Caryl said, diverted to the one subject that really interested her. "And hurry! I want to be with William!"

Chapter Seven

It was getting late in the evening when finally they set off for Raven House.

Romara was driving with Lord Ravenscar in his Phaeton, while Caryl and Alexander in the arms of his Wet-Nurse drove with the Squire.

It was, however, impossible for Romara to talk intimately with Lord Ravenscar, because the groom was sitting up behind them.

Although he might have been unable to overhear what was being said quietly, Romara was very conscious that he was there.

She knew she was excited at the thought of going home, but at the same time she was nervous and a little afraid of what Lord Ravenscar was feeling.

She could still remember what had appeared to be the angry tone of his voice when he had asked on his arrival:

"How could you do anything so damnable as to disappear like that?"

At the same time, he had kissed her!

Even to think of the touch of his lips made her heart turn over in her breast, and she felt a strange excitement rising in her throat which seemed to make her breathless.

But had it really been a kiss?

Had it meant anything more than a kind effort to calm the fear he must have seen in her face and heard in her voice?

She longed to ask what had happened when he and the Squire had seen the Chief Constable. But again she thought it would be indiscreet to talk of anything so personal in front of the groom.

She had heard Lord Ravenscar on his return tell Mrs. Coswell that they had arranged for Sir Harvey's body to be collected and for the Vicar to bury him.

Romara thought that Lord Ravenscar was anxious to prevent Mrs. Coswell from worrying or feeling distressed at having a corpse on the farm, but she had merely said sharply:

"If ye ask Oi, M'Lord, a Christian burial be too good for th' likes of 'im!"

"I agree with you," Lord Ravenscar had replied, "but at the same time, the proprieties must be observed."

Could anything be more fortunate, Romara now thought, than that Sir Harvey should have died entirely by his own fault. It was unforgivable by every code of honour to shoot at an unarmed man.

She had learnt from Caryl that it was only after she had told the Squire of Sir Harvey's threat to kidnap Alexander that he had decided to carry a pistol.

"Thank goodness you told him!" Romara had exclaimed.

"I have longed to do so for weeks," Caryl answered, "but you have been so insistent that we must keep everything secret."

"This is one occasion when I am delighted you disobeyed me!" Romara said. "But, my dearest, I was only trying to protect Alexander."

"And me," Caryl said.

She had kissed her sister on the cheek and added with a little sob in her voice:

"You saved my happiness, Romara, and I think my life too when you took me away from Sir Harvey."

"You must thank Lord Ravenscar for that."

"That I will leave to you," Caryl said. "But he will know how grateful I am. How could I be anything else when now I can marry William?"

She was so happy that Romara found it infectious, and when they heard that the gentlemen had returned they ran downstairs hand in hand, their lips smiling, their eyes alight.

They had said good-bye to Mrs. Coswell and promised to bring Alexander over to see her at the first opportunity.

Romara had remembered that they should ask if they could take the Birthday-cake with them, and she had known by the expression on Mrs. Coswell's face that she was delighted for a cake of her baking to go to Raven House.

It was therefore put carefully on the floor in the Chaise, and as the little cavalcade drove away, Farmer and Mrs. Coswell stood waving until they were out of sight.

"She was so very kind to us," Romara said in a low voice.

"You were lucky that Buxton saw you standing by the road-side waiting for the Stage-Coach," Lord Ravenscar replied.

"The Inn-Keeper brought the pony and cart back to you, I hope?" Romara asked.

"It was the only clue I had to where you might have gone," he answered.

There was a grim look on his face, which made her feel afraid.

Lord Ravenscar was obviously in a hurry to get home, and at the pace the horses were travelling it was easier not to talk.

When at last Raven House came in sight Romara felt her heart leap, and she wanted to cry out at its beauty and the joy of being back again.

"I love you," she longed to say aloud, "and I love your owner and hope to make him happy!"

She thought, however, that it was most unlikely that she would accomplish anything of the sort.

After all, what had she to offer a man who had the whole of Society from which to chose his friends, and a full and varied life without there being any necessity for him to have a wife?

Even though it was depressing to think of such

things, she could not let them sweep away her own joy at being back again.

Just as when she and Caryl had first arrived, there was a flight of white doves passing in front of them to settle on the lawn, and she looked up to see the flag moving in the breeze against the sky.

There was the Major Domo on the door-step, and Mr. Arkwright in the Hall to say with what Romara thought to be genuine feeling:

"Welcome home, M'Lady."

But there was no time to talk or to look round and they immediately went up the stairs to their bedrooms to change for dinner.

"I want my prettiest and most glamorous gown!" Caryl was saying. "William has only seen me in those old rags. What will he think when I appear in my pink tulle, or shall I wear the blue trimmed with snow-drops?"

It was a problem, and Caryl changed her mind a dozen times before finally she wore the blue because it matched her bracelet.

Romara had little time to concentrate on her own appearance.

However, Mrs. Fellows decided for her and she found when she dressed that she was wearing a white gown trimmed with camellias which made her look like a bride.

She looked at herself in the mirror and thought that perhaps Lord Ravenscar might suppose she was trying to convey a message to him, and she blushed at the thought.

But it was too late to change, and she went downstairs, conscious that she was looking her best but that every nerve in her body seemed taut and tense.

It was difficult, however, not to be relaxed at dinner when the two men vied with each other in telling stories of their childhood.

They were the same age and their mothers had been great friends, so Lord Ravenscar had really known William Buxton since they had been in their cradles.

They had been at Eton together and later at Oxford, but while Lord Ravenscar had gone into the 10th Light Dragoon Guards, William Buxton had been in the Grenadiers.

Then, because William preferred the country, while Lord Ravenscar, after his mother's death, was nearly always in London, they had met only at irregular intervals.

"I have been thinking, William," Lord Ravenscar said, "that as you have been so extremely successful with your herds, I should improve mine."

"You have certainly got the land to do so," William Buxton replied.

"That is something I want to talk to you about tomorrow," Lord Ravenscar said, "not tonight, it is too serious a subject."

William Buxton looked surprised, but he was too tactful to pursue the conversation.

When the servants left the room and they were sitting with only the lights on the table to make, as Romara had thought before, a little island in the darkness, Lord Ravenscar raised his glass.

"I am going to drink a toast," he said, "first of all to you, Caryl, because I know that you are going to be very happy with my friend William, and I think you are admirably suited to each other."

Caryl blushed and turned with a little loving gesture towards William, slipping her hand into his. Then Lord Ravenscar went on:

"Secondly, I want to drink to my wife, who has come home."

He looked at Romara as he spoke.

She thought there was an expression in his eyes which she could not understand, and a deep note in his voice which made her heart throb in a strange manner.

"Thank . . . you," she tried to say.

But somehow it was difficult for her to control her lips in the way she wished.

When dinner was over the gentlemen moved with Romara and Caryl into the Salon instead of remaining alone at the Dining-Room table.

The Butler offered them brandy and put the decanter on a side-table.

Because she felt restless and a little afraid of the strange feelings coursing within her, Romara rose to go to the window and stood looking out at the rose-garden.

It seemed a century since she had been here before, and yet, although the roses were now in full bloom, there was no other change except, she thought, in herself.

The last glow of the sun was golden on the leaping fountain and below glimmered on the quiet lake.

"It is so . . . lovely," she murmured aloud, and then a voice beside her said:

"That is why I could not understand how you could have left it—and me."

She had not known that Lord Ravenscar was beside her until he spoke.

Now he took her by the arm and drew her down to the terrace and into the garden and then started to walk across the rose-garden to the lawns.

Almost out of sight of the house was a little Greek Temple from which one could look down on the lake and see the spotted deer lying quietly under the trees in the Park.

They did not speak as they walked towards the Temple. Romara was so glad to be with him and afraid words would spoil the sense of beauty round them.

They reached the white marble seat which had been carved by Italian craftsmen.

Behind them, the classic simplicity of the Greek Temple, which some distant ancestor had brought home as a trophy, glowed like a pearl.

Romara sat down, and though she longed to look at the man beside her she stared ahead, vividly conscious of him and feeling the colour rise in her face because she knew he was looking at her.

"How could you disappear," he asked, as he had asked before, "without discussing it with me first?"

"I did not wish to . . . involve you in any more . . . trouble than I had . . . already," Romara answered.

"You were thinking of me?" Lord Ravenscar questioned.

"I thought if no-one could . . . find me and if you could . . . swear on your . . . oath that you had no idea . . . where I was, there would be no . . . trial."

"And if there had been, would you not have expected me to stand by you and help you?"

"I know you would have done so," Romara said simply, "but it would have been . . . humiliating for you and might have spoilt everything you stand for in the . . . public eye."

There was a throb in her voice and Lord Ravenscar said after a moment:

"So instead you subjected me to the misery of not knowing what had happened to you and in what trouble you might have found yourself."

"Misery?" Romara questioned in a very low voice.

"You could hardly expect me not to be concerned."

"You had been so . . . kind already, and I did not . . . want to . . . impose on you. Besides, there was . . . Caryl to think of."

"I understand that, and you were indeed fortunate that William should have appeared."

"I thank God for that every day and every night."

"How do you pray for yourself?" Lord Ravenscar asked.

She could not answer him and he saw the colour flood into her face. After a moment he said very quietly:

"Did you want to see me again?"

"I longed desperately to see . . . you and to be back at Raven House," Romara answered without thinking. "I thought of it . . . all the time."

"The house?"

The question was sharp, and now because Romara thought her response to his question had been too revealing, she could not find the words in which to reply.

"There is something I want to know, Romara," Lord Ravenscar said, "and I want you to answer me truthfully."

"You . . . know I will do . . . that."

"I have always found you very truthful," he answered, "so tell me, did you want to come back because of the house or because you wished to see me?"

She was so surprised at his question that she turned her head to look at him and found herself held spellbound by the expression in his eyes.

They sat looking at each other and Lord Ravenscar said:

"Answer me, Romara, it is important."

"I . . . wanted to . . . see . . . you," she replied, barely above a whisper, as if she could hardly obey his command.

"How much?"

"V-very . . . much. I . . . I missed . . . you."

"As I missed you."

Her eyes widened, and yet, because he held her spellbound, she could not prevent herself from asking, as he had:

"How . . . much?"

"That is one of the things I want to tell you," he said. "One of the reasons I have been trying so frantically these last weeks to find you."

"You really . . . wanted to . . . find me?"

He smiled and she thought it was because he found the question almost ridiculous.

"Do you want me to tell you," he asked in a low voice, "how empty and quiet the house seemed? How much I hated being alone here without you?"

"Without . . . me?"

He gave a sigh and then he said, looking away from her towards the lake:

"Perhaps I had better start at the beginning. There is so much to be said between us that I feel it is important we start from where, owing to my crazy, irresistible desire for revenge, we were married."

Romara felt herself trembling, but she could not take her eyes from his profile.

"I thought I was in love," Lord Ravenscar said, "and because I was conceited and over-confident, it never struck me that my love would be repulsed."

"I can . . . understand . . . that."

"It was such an utter surprise to be turned down that I behaved disgracefully. I am very ashamed of myself, Romara."

"Please . . . please do . . . not apologise . . ." she begged. "It was a shock, and anyone might do . . . strange things under such circumstances."

"Not when they are supposed to have pride and self-respect," Lord Ravenscar replied sharply.

There was silence. He did not look at her and after a moment went on:

"I know now it was not love that I felt. It was just a man's normal desire for a beautiful woman, but because I was an idealistic fool I believed she inspired in me a devotion such as I had never felt before."

Romara clenched her fingers together. It was agony to know that he felt like that about another woman, when she was longing with every fibre of her being for him to love her.

"Because," he went on, "I was not man enough to take the first set-down I had experienced in my life with dignity, you know what happened."

"Please . . . please do not . . . blame yourself," Romara said, because she could not bear the note of self-contempt in his voice. "It was . . . understandable that you should . . . be deeply hurt. But I do not want it to make you . . . bitter and . . . cynical."

"Why should you care what I feel, considering the way I treated you?" Lord Ravenscar asked.

"You have never treated me with anything but kindness and consideration," Romara replied. "But you are so . . . clever and I . . . admire you so much that I could not bear . . . anything to . . . spoil you."

"You admire me? Goodness knows why!"

Romara smiled.

"I could give you lots of reasons, but perhaps it is easier to say that everyone who knows you well . . . like those who serve you . . . thinks you are . . . everything a man and a gentleman . . . should be."

"Do you think that too?"

"You . . . know I . . . do."

Because she could not bear him to disparage himself, she went on:

"I do not think that . . . love, however much one may be . . . hurt, should ever be . . . regretted."

"Not even false love?" Lord Ravenscar asked.

"It was not false on your side, and perhaps because of it you will become . . . wiser and more . . . understanding."

"It has certainly made me wiser," Lord Ravenscar said, "and that is why I am telling you that I know now it was not real love."

He paused before he said:

"It does not compare in any way with what I feel now."

Romara drew in her breath and he turned to look at her. After a second he said slowly:

"It took me a long time to realise that what I feel for you is real love."

"What . . . are you . . . saying?" she whispered.

"I am telling you that I love you, Romara. I love you and it is completely different from anything I have ever felt in my life before."

It seemed as if a thousand lights had been lit round them and she was dazzled by the brightness of them.

Then very gently, as if he was afraid to frighten her, Lord Ravenscar put his arms round her and drew her close to him.

For one moment he looked down at her face as her head fell back against his shoulder, and then he he drew her closer still and his lips were on hers.

For a moment she could not believe it was happening.

Then the love in her heart rose like a warm wave up through her throat and into her lips.

She knew this was what she had longed for, prayed and cried for, but thought would never happen because Lord Ravenscar was in love with someone else.

It was perfect, and together they were one with the beauty all round them and yet also a part of the sky, her prayers, and all she believed was sacred.

Lord Ravenscar kissed her until she felt as if he drew her heart from between her lips and made it his.

When at length he raised his head she could only look up at him with her lips trembling and her eyes full with the glory of sunset.

"I love you," he said a little unsteadily. "And now tell me, my darling, what you feel for me."

"I love . . . you! I love . . . you!" Romara cried. "And I have done so . . . since the first moment I . . . saw you, although I did not . . . know it was . . . love."

"My precious, I wish I could say the same thing."

"How could you possibly have loved anyone who looked as I did?" Romara asked.

"But I did fall in love with you," he said, "when I came into the Salon and saw you holding the baby in your arms at the window, but like you I was not aware of it."

His arms tightened round her as he went on:

"I thought then that it seemed right for you to be standing there, and later I saw how completely you fitted into my home and were part of it."

"That is . . . what I . . . felt," Romara said, "but I never . . . thought, I never . . . dreamt, that you would . . . feel the . . . same."

"You seemed in so many ways to be like my mother," Lord Ravenscar said, "and when you waved to Arkwright and me as we rode away the day you disappeared, I knew that you belonged not only to the house but to me."

His lips were very close to hers as he said in a deep voice:

"You belong to me now and I will never let you go. I will never lose you."

"All I . . . want is to . . . stay with . . . you," Romara murmured, "to feel . . . safe, to be . . . allowed to . . . love you."

"I want your love, I want it desperately," Lord Ravenscar replied. "I know now what has always been missing in my life."

"I love you . . . I love you with . . . all of me," Romara cried, "and I have prayed every night that you might . . . love me just a . . . little, or at least have some . . . affection for me."

"What I feel for you is not a little; it is so vast, so overwhelming, that there are no words in which to describe it," Lord Ravenscar said. "I can only, my precious, show you my love."

He kissed her again and this time there was a fire in his lips that was fierce and demanding, yet at the same time it was so exciting that Romara felt as if small flames awoke inside her to flicker through her whole body.

Then as she wanted him to go on kissing her, to hold her closer and still closer, Lord Ravenscar rose to his feet, still with his arms round her.

"If you only knew," he said in a voice that had strange undertones, "since you left me, how often I have looked at that door which joins my bed-room to yours, and cursed myself for not having opened it when you were there."

"I . . . wondered if . . . you would . . . ever do so."

"You will never wonder that again," Lord Ravenscar said positively.

Then he was kissing her until the garden and the sky and the lake seemed to swim dizzily round them and she was breathless when he finally raised his head.

"We must go back to the house. We will go in by

a side-door without bothering to see William and Caryl again."

He was organising everything again in his inimitable manner and she loved him for it.

"Tonight we are going to be alone with no interruptions," he said. "Looking back, it seems to me that whenever I had anything to say to you there were always intrusions, so I never finished what I wanted to say."

"I . . . treasured every . . . moment we were . . . together."

"There will be enough of them now to stick in a thousand scrap-books," Lord Ravenscar said with a smile.

As if she could not help it, Romara moved a little closer to him.

"Is it . . . true," she asked in a voice that trembled, "that you . . . really love me? That you really . . . want . . . me?"

"That is something I am going to prove not only tonight but for the rest of our lives together," Lord Ravenscar answered.

His arms tightened round her as he added:

"I have discovered I cannot live without you, and for a very long time, my precious, we are going to stay here in the country, as I have no intention of sharing you with anyone else."

"In the country? Here in . . . the country?" Romara repeated, and there was a lilt in her voice which he did not miss.

He put his arm round her waist and turned her round so that they could begin to walk back over to Raven House.

"When I went back to London," he said, "to arrange for Hignet to bribe Sir Harvey's servants to tell us the moment the Bow Street Runners had located Caryl, I had a long talk with George Spencer."

"The Home . . . Secretary?" Romara questioned.

"Yes, and a very competent one," Lord Ravenscar answered. "He is certain, just as I am, that the war will last a long time, and it is essential on this small island that we should grow enough food to feed the whole of our population."

"So that is why you intend to increase your herd!"

"With William's help, and of course yours, my clever little wife, I intend to make this estate produce enough food not only for ourselves but at least part of London."

"I am sure . . . that will be very . . . important."

"Spencer thinks so, and so does the Prime Minister," Lord Ravenscar said, "and they have asked me not only to supervise my own land but to advise and encourage farmers all over the County."

"No-one could do it better."

"Because they wish to make it easy for me to have the right sort of authority," he went on, "and because I now have a wife who will help me, the King is to appoint me Lord Lieutenant of Buckinghamshire."

"Oh! How marvellous!" Romara cried. "You are exactly the right person to represent a King."

"I am delighted and so is the Prince," Lord Ravenscar said. "He wants all his friends in positions of power so that they can help him."

Romara turned her head to look up at him.

"You will be very . . . grand, which is just what you . . . should be, but I shall be . . . afraid that I might let you . . . down in some . . . way."

Lord Ravenscar stopped walking.

"You will not let me down," he said positively. "You will help, inspire, and advise me. That is what you have done already."

"How can you say such a . . . thing when I have been . . . nothing but a nuisance!" Romara gasped.

Lord Ravenscar looked into her eyes, and touched her hair so tenderly that it made the tears come to her eyes.

"You are lovely, yet there is so much more about you than beauty."

"Will you teach me . . . to love you . . . as you

... want to be ... loved, and how to ... excite you?"

Lord Ravenscar smiled.

"You excite me already, my precious one, more than enough for my peace of mind! But that is not what I am saying."

"Explain ... please ... explain to me."

She thought Lord Ravenscar sought for words. Then he said:

"You have reawakened in me all the ideals and all the ambitions I had when I was young. When I think of you, I want to be of service to my country and I want to do what is right and—good."

He hesitated before the last word, almost as if he felt he was revealing his inner self.

"Can I really ... do that?" Romara asked. "You are so clever ... so commanding ... I cannot believe you ... need anything I can ... give you."

"I need your love," he answered positively. "I need your gentleness, your sympathy, and your touch."

Romara drew in her breath.

"How ... wonderful ... how perfect that you should ... think like ... that."

Once again he pulled her closer to him.

"It is true, my precious one, everything I have said is true, and because of you I feel almost as if I were setting out on a Crusade."

"I will help you, I will do ... anything you want of ... me," Romara cried. "But love me ... oh! love me because I now know that without ... you and your ... love I would no longer want to ... live."

"My absurd darling!" Lord Ravenscar said the words against her lips.

Then he was kissing her possessively and demandingly and there was not only a fire on his lips but also an ecstasy that seemed to lift her from the ground.

Romara knew, as her heart beat against his heart and her soul joined with his, that their whole life together would be a Crusade.

'I adore . . . him,' she whispered in her heart. 'Please, God . . . help us.'

Then there was only the blinding, dazzling light of real love, which gives and goes on giving, without a thought of self.

ABOUT THE EDITOR

BARBARA CARTLAND, the world's most famous romantic novelist, who is also an historian, playwright, lecturer, political speaker and television personality, has now written over 200 books. She has also had many historical works published and has written four autobiographies as well as the biographies of her mother and that of her brother Ronald Cartland, who was the first Member of Parliament to be killed in the last war. This book has a preface by Sir Winston Churchill. Barbara Cartland has sold 80 million books over the world, more than half of these in the U.S.A. She broke the world record in 1975 by writing twenty books in a year, and her own record in 1976 with twenty-one. In private life, Barbara Cartland, who is a Dame of the Order of St. John of Jerusalem, has fought for better conditions and salaries for Midwives and Nurses. As President of the Royal College of Midwives (Hertfordshire Branch), she has been invested with the first Badge of Office ever given in Great Britain, which was subscribed to by the Midwives themselves. She has also championed the cause for old people and founded the first Romany Gypsy Camp in the world. Barbara Cartland is deeply interested in Vitamin Therapy and is President of the British National Association for Health.

OTHER TITLES BY BARBARA CARTLAND AND PUBLISHED BY CORGI BOOKS

WHILE EVERY EFFORT IS MADE TO KEEP PRICES LOW, IT IS SOMETIMES NECESSARY TO INCREASE PRICES AT SHORT NOTICE. CORGI BOOKS RESERVE THE RIGHT TO SHOW AND CHARGE NEW RETAIL PRICES ON COVERS WHICH MAY DIFFER FROM THOSE ADVERTISED IN THE TEXT OR ELSEWHERE.

THE PRICES SHOWN BELOW WERE CORRECT AT THE TIME OF GOING TO PRESS (NOVEMBER 78)

☐	10745 X	LOVE AND THE LOATHSOME LEOPARD	60p
☐	10744 1	A TOUCH OF LOVE	60p
☐	10786 7	NO ESCAPE FROM LOVE	50p
☐	10602 X	PUNISHMENT OF A VIXEN	50p
☐	10549 X	DUEL WITH DESTINY	50p
☐	09757 8	THE IMPETUOUS DUCHESS	40p
☐	09756 X	BEWITCHED	40p

BARBARA CARTLAND'S LIBRARY OF LOVE

☐	10543 0	THE HUNDREDTH CHANCE (No. 5)	*Ethel M. Dell*	60p
☐	10560 0	THE REASON WHY (No. 6)	*Elinor Glyn*	60p
☐	10588 0	THE WAY OF AN EAGLE (No. 7)	*Ethel M. Dell*	60p
☐	10624 0	THE VICISSITUDES OF EVANGELINE (No. 8)	*Elinor Glyn*	65p
☐	10644 5	THE BARS OF IRON (No. 9)	*Ethel M. Dell*	65p
☐	10670 4	MAN AND MAID (No. 10)	*Elinor Glyn*	65p
☐	10704 2	THE SONS OF THE SHEIK (No. 11)	*E. M. Hull*	65p
☐	10758 1	SIX DAYS (No. 12)	*Elinor Glyn*	65p
☐	10760 3	RAINBOW IN THE SPRAY (No. 13)	*Pamela Wynne*	65p

ORDER FORM

All these books are available at your bookshop or newsagent, or can be ordered direct from the publisher. Just tick the titles you want and fill in the form below.

CORGI BOOKS, Cash Sales Department, PO Box 11, Falmouth, Cornwall.

Please send cheque or postal order, no currency.

U.K. send 22p for first book plus 10p per copy for each additional book ordered to a maximum charge of 82p to cover the cost of postage and packing.

B.F.P.O. and Eire allow 22p for first book plus 10p per copy for the next six books, and thereafter 4p per book.

Overseas Customers. Please allow 30p for the first book and 10p per copy for each additional book.

NAME (block letters) ....

ADDRESS ....

....

While every effort is made to keep prices low, it is sometimes necessary to increase prices at short notice. Corgi Books reserve the right to show new retail prices on covers which may differ from those previously advertised in the text or elsewhere.